Earth-shattering news . . .

My dad pushed his chair away from the table. "Ellen. Mark. Your mother and I have something to tell you."

I tried to hold back my smile. My dad had this serious look on his face that he makes when he's trying to hide a surprise from us.

"Oh," I said slyly. "Do tell."

Maybe it was the Hawaiian vacation that I had thought about last night. Or a backyard swimming pool or the puppy Mark and I had been begging for. It would be his special way of apologizing for all the fighting we had been subjected to.

I leaned forward anxiously. My dad turned to my mom.

"Your mother and I are getting a divorce," he said.

Bantam Books in THE UNICORN CLUB series.
Ask your bookseller for the books you have missed.

THE UNICORN CLUB

ELLEN'S FAMILY SECRET

Written by
Alice Nicole Johansson

Created by
FRANCINE PASCAL

BANTAM BOOKS
NEW YORK · TORONTO · LONDON · SYDNEY · AUCKLAND

RL 4, 008-012

ELLEN'S FAMILY SECRET
A Bantam Book / January 1996

Sweet Valley High® and The Unicorn Club®
are registered trademarks of Francine Pascal

Conceived by Francine Pascal

Produced by Daniel Weiss Associates, Inc.
33 West 17th Street
New York, NY 10011

Cover art by James Mathewuse

ISBN: 0-553-48354-4
Published simultaneously in the United States and Canada

Bantam Books are published by Bantam Books, a division of Bantam
Doubleday Dell Publishing Group, Inc. Its trademark, consisting of the
words "Bantam Books" and the portrayal of a rooster, is Registered in U.S.
Patent and Trademark Office and in other countries. Marca Registrada.
Bantam Books, 1540 Broadway, New York, New York 10036.

PRINTED IN THE UNITED STATES OF AMERICA

OPM   0 9 8 7 6 5 4 3 2 1

To Jeanne and Burt Rubin

One

Some people are born to be leaders. Others are amazing athletes or actresses. And then there's the matter of intelligence, style, and looks, which either you've got or you don't. There are even some girls I know who are lucky enough to be talented and stylish at the same time (my friend Lila "I'm Perfect" Fowler, for example) or leadership oriented, artistic, and pretty all in one (the one and only Jessica Wakefield, to be exact).

Oh, and then there's me. Ellen Riteman. What are *my* virtues? If you've read about me before, do me a favor and think about it for a second. OK. Time's up.

If find yourself at a loss, guess what? You're not alone. You might have thought, Ellen had a part in that play, *Tale of a Teenage Vampire*. Oh, but she had such a hard time memorizing her lines. Or you may have said to yourself, Ellen puts in time at the day-care center. But wait, she doesn't exactly have a special touch with the kids. And even though I'm in the Unicorn Club and the Unicorns are known for being the prettiest girls at Sweet Valley Middle School, I wouldn't say my mousy brown hair and skinny legs are exactly anything to brag about.

If, for some bizarre reason, you've come up with something really incredible about me and can back it up with a concrete example, I'd appreciate you passing it on to me. I'm on a mission.

You see, when I think about myself, it's hard to find anything to be extremely proud of. My one saving grace is that I just turned thirteen. I figure I'm young, right? There's still hope that I'll discover some hidden talent as I make my way through life. Maybe one day I'll wake up with the ability to juggle flaming torches or something.

But for now, I'm basically just your average teenager, the type that doesn't stand out from the crowd. Sometimes I think I could spontaneously combust and it would take at least a week for anyone to realize I was missing. I guess eventually my mom would notice that the trash hadn't been taken out or that the cookie dough ice cream was completely untouched.

The point of telling you all this is to give you an idea why opening day of the Sweet Valley Ice Skating Rink was so important to me. My friends and I had been waiting impatiently for months (actually, it felt more like years) as we watched its construction take place in the new wing of the Valley Mall. As Lila had put it, now a perfect day at the mall would include "a little shopping, a little skating, a little eating, and a lot more shopping."

Anyway, the real reason I was so psyched about skating that Saturday afternoon was that my mom and dad had given me an absolutely gorgeous lavender skating outfit for my birthday. I had begged and pleaded for months after I spotted it in the window of Leaping Leotards. And finally, it was mine.

I had taken it out of the white tissue paper and modeled it in front of my full-length mirror at least half a dozen times in the past two weeks. But it wasn't until that day that I had an opportunity to show it off to the real world. And, well, if I'm going to be totally honest with you, I thought of it as a way to stand out from my friends for once.

You see, I wouldn't feel so ordinary if I weren't constantly surrounded by the super-extraordinary members of the Unicorn Club. Don't get me wrong, I'm proud to be a Unicorn. The Unicorns are my very best friends in the world, the girls whom I have shared the most amazing moments of my life with. The only problem is that hanging around them is sometimes this huge reminder of everything that I lack or wish for. And I must say that the jabs and jokes about me being the resident airhead or the group ditz (particularly from ultraconfident Kimberly Haver) can really bum me out.

The truth is that sometimes I say things that even *I* realize sound pretty stupid. Unfortunately, I just don't realize it until it's too late to take them back. I mean, I know I'm no rock scientist (or is it rocket scientist?) and that my grades aren't exactly wonderful, but it still seems like a little bit much when they call me a space cadet or when Jessica prances around shouting, "Ellen's out to lunch. Permanently."

Of course, the Unicorns have no idea that I get down on myself. I guess if there's one thing I'm good at, it's hiding my feelings. Like I said, the way they see me is as Ellen the ditz, good for a laugh, a pig-out session, or a shoulder to cry on. Which is kind of different from my own private personal profile of Ellen the ditz with a major inferiority complex and an imagination stuffed with unfulfilled dreams.

But slipping into my new lavender outfit in the locker room instantly made me bubble over with pride.

By the way, purple is our official club color and we always go out of our way to wear clothes in the purple family. It could be a plum-colored scrunchy (like the one Kimberly was pulling her long dark hair back with) or violet ankle socks or a pair of purple jeans. But in my case, a lavender skating outfit was a killer way to show off my Unicorn status.

The top had these tiny mother-of-pearl buttons along the back and tight lace sleeves. The skirt was a double layer of chiffon with matching lace trim along the edges. And the fit? Perfect.

I hadn't mentioned the skating outfit to my friends. I wanted it to come as a complete surprise. And just as I'd hoped, the Unicorns noticed right away.

"Ellen. Wow. I mean, that's . . . that's an excellent outfit," Lila said. She sounded almost alarmed.

I smiled at her. Lila is the most privileged (which is really just a polite way to say spoiled) girl at Sweet Valley Middle School and is used to having the best of everything. On top of living in a mansion and being chauffeured around in a shiny Rolls Royce limo, she has a charge card with unlimited credit (which answers the question: Why doesn't Lila ever wear the same thing twice?). But even Lila's skating costume, a floral print imported from Denmark, couldn't compare with the delicate fabric of mine.

"When did you get it?" Lila went on, flipping her brown hair over her shoulders.

"My birthday present," I explained nonchalantly.

"That's seriously stunning," Jessica commented as she adjusted the zipper of her purple polka-dotted skirt.

"Yeah, well," I said modestly, trying not to beam. You see, a fashion compliment from Jessica goes a long way. I figure anyone with money like Lila can dress like a top model. But with less cash to spare, Jessica has always been a trendsetter and has an incredible eye for mixing and matching.

"And check this out," I said, lifting my skates in the air to reveal Unicorn shoelaces.

Kimberly eyed the laces as she changed into her magenta leotard. "Let's not get too full of ourselves or anything."

"Let's not get too jealous because Ellen has the coolest skating outfit," Jessica retorted.

It was already clear that my birthday present was a hit with my friends. I couldn't wait another second to show off the new and improved Ellen to the rest of Sweet Valley. "I'll see you slowpokes on the ice," I said, rushing over the padded floor.

When I stepped onto the ice, the rink was filling up with people, including a lot of kids who went to Sweet Valley Middle School with us. Besides Kimberly, who's in the eighth grade, we Unicorns are all seventh-graders. I noticed Rick Hunter and Peter Jeffries, two totally cute eighth-graders, goofing off in their hockey skates.

This might sound strange, but I've always thought that Rick had gorgeous knees. And even though most people notice Peter's gorgeous smile, I think his ears are what make him really adorable. OK, maybe that's weird too, but his lobes are so small and soft-looking, I've often had the burning desire to reach out and touch them. Just chalk it up as another unfulfilled dream.

Rick and Peter waved from across the ice. *They're probably already talking about how great I look,*

I thought. I stood up straighter, lifted my chin, and waved back by wiggling my fingers in the air.

I scanned the rink and spotted Amanda Harmon and her group, the Eight Times Eight Club—eight girls who are all in the eighth grade. (Get it? Don't be embarrassed if you don't, because it took me a while to figure it out, too.) The Eights have sort of been our rivals ever since they humiliated us on the game show *Best Friends*. We always try to one-up them, and judging from the jealous glances they were firing across the ice like BB pellets, my outfit was definitely doing the job.

As I took my first strides, I instantly felt on top of the world. Well, at least on top of Sweet Valley. (Food for thought: Can you be on top of a valley?) I imagined myself as a famous Olympic skater, an American hero, warming up before her nationally broadcast routine. The skirt flowed as I began to pick up speed.

After I'd circled around a few times, I noticed Jessica skating backwards near the edge of the rink.

"Hey, Jessica," I heard Rick shout, "want to be my partner for the couples skate?"

"What about me?" Peter protested, whacking Rick's shoulder.

Jessica tilted her head, thinking.

"How 'bout both of us?" Rick suggested.

"I don't know, guys," she said, tossing her hair flirtatiously, "I'll think about it."

She turned around and skated off, leaving Peter and Rick to admire her.

"She is so awesome," Rick said dreamily.

Awesome is definitely the right choice in words. Jessica is one of those people who's awesome at every single solitary thing she does. Well, except for school. And I'm sure she could if she just set her mind to it, because her identical twin Elizabeth is a straight-A student. Jessica has blue-green eyes, a dimple in her left cheek, and shiny blond hair that I would die for.

On my next loop around I noticed that Kimberly and Lila had finally come out on the ice. I flew right past them.

"Slow down, show-off," Kimberly spouted off.

"I'm just getting warmed up," I shouted back at them with a smug smile.

Last year Kimberly's family moved away to Atlanta. She surprised us all when she suddenly came back and has been stirring up conflict ever since. The way she's always bossing people around can be a little annoying, but I have to say I pretty much admire her for it. I mean, she knows what she wants and she goes for it. But at that moment I knew that I had something that Kimberly wanted and couldn't have: the prettiest skating outfit at the entire rink.

"We'll just see how long you last at that pace," Kimberly yelled after me.

"What'd you put in your cereal this morning?" Rick asked in amazement as I whizzed by him and Peter.

I smiled to myself. Somehow, being in that outfit made me feel like a better skater than I ever had. I felt as if I could do anything I set my mind to. Maybe I had finally discovered my virtue—my hidden talent as a skating prodigy.

There was a jump I had seen Lila and Jessica do at the old rink downtown. They would twist in the air, their arms held above their head like a ballerina, and land on one foot, extending the back leg. I'm not the perfect judge or anything, but I'd noticed that Jessica always wobbled on her landing and Lila had this funny habit of overextending her arms on her takeoff. She also made this totally ridiculous face when she finished, sucking in her cheeks like she thought she was a princess or something.

As I sped past other skaters, I knew I could nail the jump and draw the spotlight on myself. My jump would be the tightest and most professional the Unicorns had ever seen. They would be amazed to learn that I had been hiding my gift from them for all these years.

I glided along the ice, psyching myself up, and making sure that all the Unicorns had spotted me. *Show your stuff, Ellen*, I said to myself.

I reached the corner of the ice and kicked up my right leg, just the way I had seen Jessica do it a million times before. In an instant, I was airborne. I twirled my body around holding my arms tightly over my head. The next thing I knew, I had landed. Splat!

But not on one skate as I had planned. I had fallen

on my behind and slid across the ice, like a hockey puck spinning out of control. As I reached out my hands to stop myself, I felt a hot flash rush through my body.

I looked down and closed my eyes, trying to hold back the tears that wanted to flow from them. My palms stung from scraping against the ice, and my thigh throbbed from the impact of the fall. But on the inside I felt a worse kind of pain. You see, embarrassment hurts more than any bruise or skinned knee or blood blister or bee sting or stubbed toe I've ever gotten. Bear with me and you'll get a good example of why this is so.

"Ellen! Ellen!" I heard Jessica cry out.

I twisted my body around to see my three friends rushing across the ice to my rescue, making so much noise that practically everyone on the rink seemed to be staring.

"Should we call an ambulance?" Lila shrieked as she skidded to a stop directly in front of me.

Leave it to Lila to be overly dramatic. "I'm OK," I insisted, immediately pulling myself off the ice. "I just slipped, it's no biggy."

"That was no slip, Ellen," Kimberly corrected. "That was a major wipeout. You could have broken your collarbone or something."

"But I'm OK." I grabbed on to Jessica's shoulder to regain my balance. "See?"

"You're sure?" Lila asked, putting on her serious face. "Soft-tissue damage is very hard to diagnose.

You just might not realize it yet but you may have to see a physical therapist or have some laser surgery."

"It's kind of you to give your opinion, Dr. Fowler, but I thought you were an expert on foot *wear*, not foot *care*," Kimberly said, rolling her eyes. "And if Ellen says she's fine, she's fine. Right?"

"Right," I said firmly, stumbling a little as I shook out my legs.

And that's when the laughter began. Sometimes, when someone hurts themselves, you hold in your laughter until you realize that they're OK. At least that's what seemed to be happening here.

"You must have skid one hundred feet on your butt!" Jessica said through snorts of laughter.

"A little farther to the left and you would've mowed down the Eights," Lila added, grinning.

"Interesting form, Ellen," Peter said as he passed by with Rick. "I'd give you a one point five three."

Rick and Peter had seen! Why me?

Rick skated backwards and circled around us. "Too bad I didn't have my video camera. We could have submitted it to one of those sports blooper shows."

As the boys skated on, I just wanted to disappear. The idea of spontaneous combustion suddenly sounded kind of appealing. Poof! I'd disintegrate into a cloud of purple smoke. But unfortunately, I was still one hundred percent there. And by this point, Jessica, Lila, and Kimberly were laughing so hard, it looked like they were going to cry.

"I haven't laughed this much since you slipped

with your tray in the cafeteria and got mashed potatoes and gravy in your hair," Jessica gasped.

Another memorable moment in the history of Ellen Riteman and her bouts with uncoordination. And in case you're wondering, no, my hair hasn't looked the same since.

"I guess a happening outfit can't exactly cover for the fact that you're a complete klutz." Kimberly giggled as she reached for the railing.

"They even flub up in the Olympics sometimes," I pointed out weakly as I moved over to the edge.

"Not on easy jumps like that." Lila put her hands on her hips. "Your feet crossed at the totally wrong place. Maybe you need private lessons."

"Plus, you need to become more graceful before you can pull off a move like that," Jessica rattled on. "You might need to take ballet lessons."

"But grace isn't something you can learn," Kimberly piped in. "Either you've got it or you don't."

I felt my face turn red. Suddenly I missed some of the ex-members of the Unicorn Club. A couple weeks before, half of the group had gone splitsville because of "irreconcilable differences" and formed a new group called the Angels. Kimberly and Lila kept telling me it wasn't a major loss, but now I really wished someone nice like Mary Wallace or Jessica's twin sister, Elizabeth, were around. And Mandy Miller definitely would have told everyone off for teasing me.

"I don't need special lessons," I protested. "It was just an accident."

"Well, if you're planning to try it again, you just have to do it a little more like this," Jessica said and then zoomed off.

I watched as Jessica skated toward the opposite corner of the ice. Then she kicked her leg into the air and floated up and around. It was a perfect jump. Her landing wasn't even wobbly, as I had remembered.

Jessica curtsied, and Lila and Kimberly cheered as she cruised back.

"Ten! Ten!" Peter hollered from across the rink.

Rick whistled loudly.

"Maybe you should make up a routine and get in a local competition," Kimberly suggested enthusiastically as Jessica rejoined us. "You're a natural."

I should have expected all of this to happen. Whom was I trying to fool? The best outfit in the rink couldn't magically transform me into the best skater. The best skater was none other than my friend with the sparking eyes and flowing blond hair. The super-talented and mega-extraordinary Jessica Wakefield was, as usual, the star.

Jessica was in the middle of another curtsy when she pointed at my outfit and frowned. "Wait. Hold the compliments. Is that a rip?"

"A rip?" I repeated. Somehow in my confusion I couldn't make any sense of what she was saying.

Lila and Kimberly twisted their heads back toward me.

"Did you just totally destroy the coolest skating outfit in the history of the world?" Lila squeaked, stepping back and looking at me from head to toe.

Kimberly grabbed on to the fabric. "Ellen? Look! You ruined it."

Now their words had sunk in. I whipped my head down to check out the damages. I couldn't believe what I saw. The entire front layer of the chiffon was shorn and little strings hung from it. I guess we had been huddled so closely that nobody had noticed before.

"It's no big deal," I said, trying to cover the tear with my hands. "Really," I added as firmly as I could manage. On top of being an uncoordinated joke I wasn't about to let my friends think I was a big baby. "These things happen."

Kimberly nodded. "To you they obviously do."

"And that must have been really expensive. Your parents will kill you," Jessica added.

My parents! They had made such a big deal about splurging on something while I was still growing. How could I tell them I'd ruined my skating skirt after a measly five minutes on the ice?

"Maybe your parents will buy you a new one," Lila said.

I grimaced. They would never dream of buying me a new one. I would have to make the money myself and replace it before they found out. Wait a minute—whom was I kidding? I'd spend the rest of my adolescence baby-sitting before I could afford a new skating outfit. My only option was to fix it on my own.

"They won't need to buy me a new one," I said, trying to sound confident. "I'm an expert seamstress." I shouldn't have said expert, but it just kind of came out.

"You?" Lila uttered dubiously, examining the rip more closely.

"Sure," I retorted. "I'm just a regular Betty Crocker."

Kimberly shook her head. "She's a cook, Ellen, not a seamstress. Duh."

"Oh, well, still. I sew things all the time."

"Like what?" Jessica asked suspiciously.

"Like lots of things," I fibbed. "This will be a piece of cake."

Well, I *had* sewn a button on a blouse before. And, I mean, how hard could it be to mend a little rip? With my mom's sewing machine I could definitely make the outfit as good as new. Well, at least almost as good.

"Next time you see me in this, you won't even be able to deflect a taw," I assured them.

Kimberly smirked. "I think you mean de*tect* a *fl*aw. And I'll believe it when I see it."

I blushed. "Detect a flaw," I repeated, not surprised that I had gotten tongue-twisted. That happens sometimes when I get nervous or upset. "I'll get to work as soon as I get home," I said, putting on my biggest smile. But the truth was, I didn't want to go home to sew. What I wanted to do was plop on my bed with a carton of ice cream and cry until my next birthday.

"Personally, I just wish you hadn't wiped out in front of Amanda and those crazy Eights," Lila complained.

"One Unicorn looks bad and we all take a blow," Kimberly agreed. "They were howling when they saw you wipe out."

"At least we got a good laugh, too," Jessica said.

"Yeah, too bad you couldn't see yourself flying all over the place. You looked like a circus performer," Kimberly said. My friends cracked up so hard, they nearly tipped over.

I gulped as I followed them off the ice. Why did they have to rub it in? And why did the last laugh always have to be on me?

Two

On Monday morning, I seriously considered going to school with a brown bag over my head.

Gossip about a student at Sweet Valley Middle School spreads faster than the chicken pox in a kindergarten classroom. I was positive that word had gotten out about my wipeout at the ice rink and had already funneled through the rumor mill. Jessica had obviously told Elizabeth, who must have passed it on to the other Angels. Meanwhile, Rick Hunter probably blabbed to Jake Hamilton, who probably had bumped into Caroline Pearce (our resident gossip columnist) at Casey's ice cream parlor and told her. Caroline must have passed it on to Mr. Clark, our principal, who maybe even called an emergency meeting to inform the entire faculty. OK, I'm exaggerating about Mr. Clark, but not about anyone else.

And speaking of exaggeration, that's exactly what happens to any little rumor that travels around school. I was worried that what started as a spill on the ice would turn into a story about how I was whisked away by paramedics and was in surgery all weekend. Maybe kids would even say I'd never walk again.

But at least once they saw me bouncing down the hall on my way to first period, everyone would know the truth. How bad could the fall have been if I wasn't even limping?

So instead of a paper bag, I put on my favorite purple sweater and my perfectly worn-in jeans with the daisy patches on the knees, and I said to myself over and over, *It's not exactly the end of the world.* I mean, sooner or later people would probably get tired of talking about my spill. By the time I got to Sweet Valley High School, anyway.

"Hey, Ellen!" Mandy Miller yelled as she ran to catch up with me.

My heart sank with dread. Normally, I was glad to see Mandy. Even though she isn't officially a Unicorn anymore, she's stayed friends with all of us. She's nice, funny, and the funkiest dresser you've seen. Today, for instance, she had on a men's checkered blazer and a red tie with a pair of oversized black jeans.

But I didn't want to listen to her make a big deal about my fall. "So you heard?" I said, squinching my forehead.

"Yeah, I can't wait to go check out the rink next weekend. I talked to Jessica last night and she told me you guys had an amazing time." Mandy loosened her tie.

I looked at Mandy skeptically. She was so thoughtful, she was probably holding herself back from mentioning the disaster.

"And, well, you know. Did she tell you anything else?" I asked cautiously.

Mandy thought for a second. "Oh, yeah, that the guy at the snack-bar cash register is too gorgeous for words. Jessica said he looks like a mixture of Johnny Buck and . . . um . . ."

"Tommy Rivera," I filled in. Johnny Buck is the hottest living rock star and Tommy is an eighth-grader with short brown hair and perfect teeth. Lila had actually been the one to point out the bizarre fusion of looks.

"Oh. Here's my class." Mandy pointed to a doorway. "I'll see you later."

I waved and walked on toward my homeroom, my stomach in knots. Mandy was nice enough not to embarrass me, but not many other kids were as thoughtful.

"Hey, Ellen," Randy Mason said as he came toward me.

I stopped in my tracks and put my hands on my hips. "Just say it, OK? Just give it to me. Let's get this over with. Now."

Randy raised his eyebrows. "I just wanted to ask you if you had a good weekend."

"Me?" I asked in astonishment.

"Yes, you." Randy looked perplexed as he moved toward his locker. "I'm sorry I asked."

"Oh, no. It's OK," I said, almost stunned. "It's just . . . forget it."

Randy shook his head and dialed his combination.

Finally I saw Jessica and Lila racing down the corridor together. I braced myself for the inevitable abuse.

"So," Jessica said, planting herself by my side. "Are you all set for the meeting?"

"The meeting?" I repeated. Was I hearing clearly? No mention of the rink, my tattered outfit, the whole spectacle? I guess it wasn't as huge a deal as I had built it up in my mind. It seemed practically forgotten.

"Yoo-hoo? Ellen?" Lila said, leaning close and waving her hand in front of my face. "Earth to Ellen. You are aware that you agreed to hold the meeting at your house?"

I exhaled with relief. I had been so preoccupied by the mishap that I hadn't even gotten excited about hosting the Unicorn meeting after school.

"Oh, yeah, I'll be set," I told them.

I suppose it would have been nice if they had asked me about my leg and if I had gotten a big bruise. (Yes, if you're wondering, I had. It was the size and color of an eggplant.) Or about the state of my skating skirt (which was crumpled in a ball underneath my socks, if you care to know). But I was so glad that there was no mention of my tumble that I couldn't actually complain.

"Good munchies?" Jessica asked.

"My mom's making seven-layer bars," I answered.

"Just make sure you lock that little brat in his room before we get there," Lila joked.

Lila was talking about Mark, my ten-year-old brother. He's a drag to have around during meetings . . . or during meals, on the weekend, or on vacation. Get the picture? He's in that pesty phase.

"Taken care of," I promised.

I had already arranged with my mom for Mark to play with his friend Jim down the street till dinnertime. It was always exciting to host a meeting, and I definitely wanted it to run smoothly.

"This meeting will come to order," Kimberly said sternly.

We were sitting in the living room, stuffing our faces with seven-layer bars and this incredible punch that my mom makes with raspberry sherbet.

"Oh, yes, this meeting will come to order," Lila repeated, pushing her snack aside.

Jessica cleared her throat. "This meeting will come to order."

I looked at my friends, confused. "I thought that until we made a decision about the presidency, the person who hosted the meeting was acting president."

This was actually the real reason that the meeting was being held at my house that day. Until we picked a new president, we had agreed to have meetings on neutral territory. And since I was the only one not in the running, the meetings were automatically held here.

Lila sighed. "All right, then. Just go ahead, Ellen. Let's get with it so we can pick a real president."

"This meeting will come to order," I said, with a flourish. After all, if this was my chance to be king for the day, I was going to enjoy it. "I guess the first item on the agenda is the ultracritical matter of the presidency."

The sad thing was that we'd gone through the ordeal of picking a president earlier in the year. Last year, the Unicorn president was Janet Howell, who went on to Sweet Valley High and left us presidentless.

With Janet gone, Lila and Jessica were both dead set on assuming the honored position and declared a dare war to determine the winner. Needless to say, the whole thing turned out to be a megadisaster and we ended up realizing that it had brought out the *worst* in all of us. At least that's what Mandy Miller had said. She reminded us that the Unicorn Club should be a club that brought out the *best* in its members. In a split second we all nominated her to be our president. And it was an excellent choice. But then, unfortunately, the club got torn apart and Mandy sided with the Angels.

So once again the Unicorns had to pick a new president. And of the four of us, I was the only one who wasn't vying for the job. I think it's pretty obvious that I'm not president material. But I felt torn apart over who was best suited for the job. The problem was that Jessica, Lila, and Kimberly were all born to be leaders. Not followers.

Lila's father is the president of Fowler Industries, and I know his management techniques have worn off on her. Lila really understands how important image is to the success of a group and is constantly suggesting ways for us to "function more effectively."

On the other hand, Jessica embodies what it means to be a Unicorn. She's confident, popular, and always the life of the party. There's something about Jessica's personality that automatically makes you look up to her. And let's face it, she puts the club before school, homework, family, and chores. A true Unicorn diehard.

But then there's Kimberly. When Kimberly Haver talks, people listen. She loves to goof around, but when it's time for business, it's time for business. She can make this incredibly loud whistle by sticking her fingers in her mouth and can bring a meeting to order when things are getting out of control.

With three amazing candidates, how would we ever pick one president? How would any of them agree to give it up? And how would we ever get anywhere as a group if this was all we ever worried about?

"Maybe we don't really need a president," I suggested, perking up in my seat.

"Don't need a president?" Lila coughed.

"Really, Ellen, what kind of lame idea is that?" Jessica asked, frowning.

I sank back into the couch, wanting to take it back.

But Kimberly wouldn't let the matter drop. "We'll become an anarchy," she protested.

"What's that?" Jessica asked.

I was glad she asked, because I didn't have a clue and I don't like admitting to things I don't know about. That usually prompts a lot of jokes about how I have air in my head.

Kimberly cleared her throat. "Anarchy means the complete absence of government. It leads to political disorder and violence. Don't you guys listen in class?" Kimberly added.

"And since when are *you* a history scholar?" Jessica asked.

"Well, if I'm going to be president, I want to keep up my grades and set a good example," Kimberly said breezily.

Lila rolled her eyes. "I don't know about *that*, but Kimberly's right about needing a president. Management is what keeps an organization up and running. My father says that's the key to his success."

"Plus the Unicorns need to have a person who will be designated to speak on their behalf," Jessica said with a smile that said "And I'm that person." She turned to me. "Just because you don't have what it takes to be president, doesn't mean we don't need one, Ellen."

"Forget I said it," I pleaded. "Of course we need a president."

"And if we go with me, my dad will definitely give us some extra perks. Like for starters we could hold meetings in his boardroom," Lila said with a smug grin.

"That's called bribery, Lila," Kimberly retorted. "You know what *that* means, don't you? You should be disqualified from the running just on principle."

"She does have a point, Lila," Jessica piped in.

"Give me a break!" Lila shouted.

"Cool it, you guys," I said desperately. "I think there's a more important item on the agenda today, anyway."

"Until we figure this out, we're barely even a club," Kimberly hissed.

"Yeah. What could be more important than the presidency?" Lila snapped.

"Family Day," I replied with a smile.

Family Day was an annual event sponsored by Sweet Valley Middle School, held at Green Lake Forest. We all took our parents, packed picnic lunches, and spent the afternoon hanging out on the lake, playing games and letting our parents mingle (or whatever it is that parents do).

"Family Day?" Jessica repeated, a twinkle in her eye. "I absolutely can't wait!"

It was like mentioning chocolate to chocolate lovers. The topic of the presidency was dropped so quickly, it was as if a tornado had swept it away.

"I've already picked out my outfit," Lila said boastfully. "It's a short, flowy sundress. Countryish yet contemporary."

Jessica and I exchanged glances. When Lila talks about her latest wardrobe additions, none of us can compete. We just sit back and listen.

"You'll die when you see the beautiful straw hat that goes with it," Lila went on. "And my father and I are having our meal catered by Josephena's. Lots of finger foods. Caviar, shrimp cocktail, and crab flown in from Maryland."

Jessica looked at Lila stubbornly. "I'm sure it'll be fine, Lila, but *nothing* compares to my dad's barbecued chicken. He's bringing the hibachi, and we're going to have the hugest feast."

"What's a picnic without a big turkey sandwich and some grapes?" Kimberly chimed in. "Plus you wouldn't believe this gorgeous basket that my mom bought. It has a red and white checkered blanket and matching red plates and cups."

"What about you, Ellen?" Lila asked. "What's on your menu?"

I felt a flutter of anxiety. I hadn't anticipated that

question. "Um, well," I began. You see, every time I mentioned Family Day to my parents they just brushed me off. My mom had said, "Let's talk about that later" about seventeen times already.

"Well?" Lila pressed.

"Potato salad and biscuits," I said quickly. Those were the first foods that came to mind.

"And what else? That's not exactly lunch," Kimberly pointed out. "You need a main course."

"Oh, right." I cleared my throat. "Well, we still have to decide."

I was about to mention how great my mom's potato salad was when I heard voices erupt from the kitchen.

"I don't want to hear it!" I heard my dad yell. "I am not in the mood for being reprimanded."

"But how could you forget to bring a measly carton of milk home?" my mom asked. "I must have reminded you five times."

I gulped as I noticed my friends' nervous expressions. Lila stared at the table. Jessica stared at Lila. Kimberly stared at me! My whole body tensed up.

"I've got a lot on my mind, Nancy," he yelled back. "Milk is not exactly high on my priority list."

"This is not just about a carton of milk and you know it, Hank!"

I squirmed on the couch. My parents seemed to be having these fights on a daily basis. I was used to their fighting in front of me and Mark. But in front of my friends? I was mortified. I gritted my teeth and did the only thing I could think of. I pretended that everything was OK.

"Just a little lovers' quarrel," I said casually. "Anyway, what are you going to wear to the picnic, Lila?"

"Ellen, I, I . . ." Lila sounded uneasy. "I just described it."

"Oh, yeah. Duh." I slapped my palm against my forehead. "I was thinking about wearing my purple overalls with . . . hmmm, any suggestions?"

My friends looked at me blankly. And then the voices escalated again.

"And what do you think the kids are going to pour in their cereal?" my mom demanded. "Orange juice?"

"I said I'd go after dinner, Nancy. And I will," he responded in this angry but restrained tone that my dad uses when he's trying not to explode through the roof.

Kimberly pushed back her chair. "Look, Ellen? I think we better leave."

"I second that motion," Lila said, quickly gathering her things.

"What?" I was not about to blow my rare opportunity to act as leader of the crowd. "But I'm running this meeting, and it won't end until I officially say it does. We should go back to the matter of the presidency," I insisted, trying to show them that everything was A-OK.

"I just didn't realize how late it was." Kimberly

twisted her wrist to check a watch that wasn't really there.

"But—there are still four items on the agenda," I argued.

"But I have to get home to help my mom make a tuna casserole and clean up around the house," Jessica said, tucking a wisp of hair behind her ear.

Chores? Was this meeting such a disaster that Jessica Wakefield would rather do chores? "But, but . . . you always pick the Unicorns first!"

Jessica looked down as she adjusted the straps on her purple backpack.

Kimberly swung her book bag over her shoulder. "Call you later," she said quickly.

"You guys!" I protested as they filtered out of the room and tiptoed past the kitchen to the front door.

I buried my face in my hands. They were leaving, and there was nothing I could do about it. My parents' obnoxious argument had succeeded in making me the worst hostess in Unicorn history. I'd be lucky if my friends would ever come to my house for another meeting.

"I'm sick of being the one who takes all the responsibility around here," my mom shouted, back in the throes of an argument.

"Do you want the neighbors to overhear us?" my dad snapped, even louder. "Lower your voice."

"Yeah, lower your voice," I muttered. But unfortunately, it was a little too late for that.

Three

"Last week you said you'd fix the roof," my mom yelled.

I gripped the arm of the sofa. I was still sitting in the living room, stunned as I listened to my parents argue over a million different things. They covered filing income taxes, finding a new gardener, dealing with car insurance, and were now going back and forth on, well, you heard it—the roof. They had this weird rhythm going. As my dad got more angry, my mom calmed down. Then my dad would say something to trigger my mom. She'd get really hysterical and my dad would suddenly chill out.

"Last week I may have said I'd fix the roof. I just didn't say when I would get to it," my dad replied calmly.

It was true. I remembered that conversation, which

wasn't exactly a trip to the amusement park either.

"But there's a leak in Ellen's room," my mom protested. "And before another rainstorm, I want you to get up there, Hank."

I took a deep breath and stood up. I didn't care about that little leak in my ceiling, so why should they? Cautiously I opened the kitchen door and eased my way in.

"The rainy season's months away," my dad was saying, his arms folded. "And whatever made you think that I knew how to fix a roof?"

I coughed softly.

Both my parents turned to me, looking startled.

Then my mom's face relaxed into a smile. "Ellen!" she exclaimed cheerfully.

My dad grinned, too. "Hey, El."

"Hi," I responded nervously.

"Have a nice day?" my dad asked, kissing me on the forehead.

"It was, well . . ." I looked back and forth between my parents. They didn't look angry or mad. It was as if nothing was wrong.

"Everything OK, sweetheart?" my mom asked.

"Well, yeah," I began, feeling flustered. "It's just— I couldn't help overhearing that thing about the roof. And, well, I just came in here to tell you that it's not a big deal. It's a tiny leak, and if I put a bowl out, it doesn't make a mess or anything. I actually kind of like it. It makes me feel, you know, close to nature."

"Ellen, there's no reason that you should have a

leak in your bedroom," my mom explained, still smiling a little. "Not to mention that if we don't repair it now the damages could get worse."

My dad cracked his knuckles. "Not that I don't have able hands, I just think it's a job for professional roofers." He put on his goofiest grin. "Not a dentist."

"I guess that would be like asking a handyman to give a fluoride treatment," my mom joked, and my dad chuckled.

I frowned. Had I just imagined that my parents were angry at each other? I mean, maybe it only seemed that way. Maybe they just got a little carried away talking about household responsibilities, which you have to admit isn't the most fun topic no matter how you slice it.

"Hungry?" my mom asked me.

"Why don't we order out?" my dad suggested.

"Good idea, honey," my mom said, collapsing into a chair. She looked at me. "Whatever you want, El."

Honey? I repeated to myself. Not exactly a nickname you use when you're annoyed with someone.

"What do you say? Chinese? Italian?" My dad pulled a few take-out menus from the top of the refrigerator. "Mmm. How about this new hamburger place that Mark's been wanting to try?"

I sighed with relief. There was no doubt about it—my parents weren't really angry at each other after all. Of course, it was a major bummer that the Unicorns had overheard what had *sounded* like an argument. But it was obviously not that big a deal. There are kinks in every marriage, right? My parents were just having a heated discussion. Once I explained this to my friends they'd probably just giggle and say, "You should see my mom and dad going at it. I'm glad to know that your parents are human, too."

"How about Chinese?" I requested, feeling better by the minute. "Egg rolls and moo-shu vegetables would be excellent. Oh, and some fried rice."

My mom took the menu and dialed the phone number on the corner of the sheet. "Yes, hello. I'd like to make an order to be delivered."

"How about some Kung Pao chicken?" my dad suggested, licking his lips.

My mom nodded and placed the order.

"Hey, El, I forgot to ask you about the skating outfit. How'd it go over with the gang?" my dad asked.

I bit my lip. Maybe this was my opportunity to 'fess up, since my parents were in such good moods. My mom would bring me cookies and milk (well, I guess I'd have to settle for orange juice) and tell me a story about tripping in front of the student body and ripping her favorite jeans when she was in junior high. My dad would put his arms around me and offer to take me to the mall tomorrow to replace the skirt.

But then again, there was a definite risk. I would be taking a chance of letting them get mad again. Really mad. But this time, at me.

"Well?" my dad pressed.

I imagined a lecture about taking care of expensive

things and another about never trying out stunts on the ice (or the ski slopes, a diving board, Rollerblades, or a bike) that were beyond my level of skill. Even the thought of it was too much to bear.

"To tell you the truth, I've never gotten so much attention in my entire life," I said truthfully. "I don't think there was a person in the rink that didn't notice me."

"See, Nancy, I knew it was worth spending the extra money on something Ellen would enjoy so much," my dad said. "I'd love to come down to the rink and watch you in action."

My heart started to pound. For obvious reasons, this was not exactly an option. "Um, well, that's a great idea, only, well, don't plan to come too soon. I, um, I . . . I need a little more practice."

"You just let us know when you're ready," my mom said.

"I will. I mean, it might not be for a while." I smiled as innocently as I could. "And I think I'm going to go to my room and do some homework before the food comes."

"Good for you," my mom replied. "We'll call you when it gets here."

I dashed out of the room and up the stairs. It was about time I took up my job as a seamstress.

Forget the sewing machine, I thought as I examined all the knobs and pedals and wires. The machine looked harder to maneuver than a stick shift on a steep hill. I figured I'd probably have better luck mending my skirt by hand.

I sneaked my mom's sewing kit from the hall closet and rushed into my room. Opening the top drawer of my dresser, I dug the skirt out from underneath my collection of mismatched socks.

I sat down on my bed and examined it closely. Ugh! Little hairs from the chiffon sprung out from the torn fabric. The rip extended the entire length of the skirt. It was even worse than I had remembered.

I started by trimming away the stray strings with a sharp pair of scissors. Then I held it out. Amazingly, the outfit already looked better. Maybe I had found my true hidden talent. Maybe Mandy Miller and I would someday become a famous designing team and create our own line of skating apparel.

All I had left to do was to stitch up the rip. And how hard could that be? I had already proven to be a master with the scissors. By the weekend I'd be cruising (very cautiously) around the Sweet Valley Ice Rink in my lavender costume, getting compliments from all the other skaters. Maybe my mom and dad could come and watch me, after all.

I looked at the different colors of thread in my mom's assortment. There were spools of green, black, white, red, and a few shades of blue. No lavender. But thread is thin. Who would ever really notice if the match wasn't exactly right? And the royal blue was *pretty* close. I selected a fine needle and unspooled a long piece of thread, then started to slip it through the hole.

"Ouch!" I squeaked, pricking my finger with the needle.

So that's what thimbles are for, I thought as I sucked on my pointer finger for a second and slipped a little silver case over it. Finally I was ready to begin.

I carefully pulled the thread through the delicate fabric. I made about three stitches, but the chiffon got a little snagged. I flattened it out and went on with a few more loops. It didn't look so good, but hey, it was a work in progress. Once I'd made the preliminary stitches, I could go back and improve it.

Suddenly I heard a loud voice filter up from downstairs. My heart started pounding. Were my parents fighting again?

I threw down the skirt, jumped up, and opened my door.

"Ellen!" my dad yelled.

I stepped into the hallway. "What is it?" I asked as my stomach filled with butterflies.

"Dinner's here," my mom yelled.

I giggled to myself. Why was I so jumpy?

I closed my door and trotted down the staircase two steps at a time. Seamstresses, after all, have to eat, too.

Four

When I got to school on Tuesday morning, I saw the Unicorns gathered by the water fountain. It looked as if they were whispering about something. I rushed down the hall, psyched to join the gossip session.

"Hey, you guys!" I greeted them.

Lila snapped her head around and nudged Jessica, who was still talking.

"Hey, Ellen," Jessica said stiffly.

"Good morning," Kimberly added politely.

"What were you guys talking about?" I asked, leaning up against the wall. "Anything I should know about?"

They all gave each other funny looks.

"The day-care center," Lila spit out.

"English homework," Kimberly said at the same time.

"Family Day," Jessica said on top of them.

Jessica cleared her throat. "Actually, see, we were talking about how we're so excited about Family Day, but that we have to put in some time at the day-care center and finish our English homework before we can go," she said in one big breath.

Lila nodded eagerly. "Yeah, that's it exactly."

"Exactly," Kimberly repeated.

I looked at them suspiciously.

"So what *are* we going to do about all that English homework?" Lila sighed.

I folded my arms. Talk about phony! "If you guys are trying to hide something from me, don't."

"Hide something?" Lila looked at me innocently.

"Us?" Jessica yelped.

As my friends stood there with fake-looking smiles, my stomach started churning. One thing was clear—they had been talking about me! They had been complaining about yesterday's disastrous meeting and were trying to cover it with this ridiculous excuse.

"OK, you guys, admit it. You were talking about the meeting yesterday," I said flatly.

Lila's eyes widened. "Why would we be talking about you?"

I took a deep breath. "I know it sounded like my parents were fighting, but they weren't really. They were just having a discussion. You guys just over-reacted and rushed out and didn't give me a chance to explain. I know your parents argue, too.

It's normal to argue. It's, like, abnormal not to argue, and besides—"

"Ellen, we weren't talking about the meeting," Jessica broke in.

I looked at her doubtfully. I was a little out of breath from babbling. "Really?" I asked softly.

"Not even," Lila added firmly.

"Oh," I said wearily.

"I'm sorry we left in such a rush without helping you clean up the living room or anything," Kimberly put in. "It was uncool."

"But now that you mention it, Ellen," Lila said, "I was thinking about the meeting and I realized that hosting two in one week is a huge responsibility." She leaned over and took a drink from the water fountain.

"She's right, Ellen," Kimberly agreed. "No one's ever done it before."

Jessica nodded. "It's a lot to ask."

My face heated up. So my friends *were* freaked out by how my parents were fighting—so freaked out that they didn't trust me to host another meeting.

"But . . . but what about our agreement to have meetings on neutral territory?" I asked.

"That was just a stupid idea," Kimberly replied, waving her hand in the air dismissively.

"It puts all the burden on you, Ellen. It could be months before we agree on a president," Jessica pointed out.

"We could have the Wednesday meeting at my house," Lila offered.

"Or my house," Jessica said enthusiastically.

"Or mine," Kimberly added.

"But my mom is already counting on it," I said desperately. How could I give up my chance to host the next meeting? Once my friends saw that there was really nothing the matter with my family, I'd get my credibility as a Unicorn back. "She told me she's looking forward to it. You can't back out." I could feel my temperature rising and my jaw tensing up. "And I really, really, really, really want to have the meeting at my house. I mean—"

Kimberly gripped my arm. "Chill out, Ellen. If it's that important to you we'll do it."

"We were just looking out for you. But it's fine with me," Jessica added wearily.

I let out my breath. "Then it's settled. Meeting as planned. My house. Wednesday. Be there."

Holding the meeting at my house suddenly felt more important than it ever had. I wanted to show them that even though I wasn't running for president, I was a dedicated Unicorn like them. I wanted them to remember that I could run a meeting as efficiently as Kimberly. I wanted them to see that I had a flair for hosting like Lila and Jessica. And most important, I wanted them to realize that everything was fine between my parents.

"We need to talk about Family Day," I said that night at dinner. It seemed like the right time to bring it up. My mom was quietly picking at her salad, my dad was on his second portion of lasagna, and Mark was spilling his food all over the place.

"Family Day?" my mom asked. "When is it?"

I frowned. "I've told you a million times, Mom. It's on Sunday. We need to pack a picnic lunch like last year. I'll go to the grocery store with you and help pick everything out."

"That'll be fine, Ellen," my mom replied.

"But we need to plan the menu first," I went on, "so we know what to buy. Lila is having this catered meal flown in from Maryland or something, and Jessica's dad is bringing the hibachi for a barbecue. I want to do something special, too."

My mom look flustered. "How about I make my famous buttermilk biscuits, fried chicken, and potato salad?"

"Perfect," I answered. It sounded like good home cooking, the way a family picnic should be. But my dad didn't seem too interested. He was just staring at his plate. "What do you think, Daddy? Any dessert requests?"

"Huh?" My dad looked up.

"Anything you'd like me and mom to make for the picnic?" I asked. "For dessert?"

"Oh. Whatever you like," he mumbled.

I looked at him curiously for a second, but decided not to be insulted. I mean, I guess dads will eat pretty much anything you put in front of them. And I mean *anything*. My dad has always been good for getting rid of burnt cookies, pizza crust, and leftover vegetables on my dinner plate. So I was sure that whatever my mom and I prepared, it would be a hit.

"Jim Wedaa got a new bike," Mark blurted out.

"Well, good for him," my mom said.

"And I want one, too," Mark added. "It's a mountain cruiser with, like, twenty-five speeds. And it's Day-Glo green."

"You got a new bike last Christmas, honey," my mom reminded him.

"Compared to this, mine's not even a bike," Mark complained. "It's a tricycle for a baby."

"I'll tell you what, Mark, why don't we go to the bike shop this weekend and check it out together," my dad suggested. "I'm sure I can work something out."

"Awesome!" Mark was beaming. "Wait till I tell Jim."

My mom looked at my dad in disbelief. "Hold on, Hank. Mark cannot get another new bike. He'll expect a new one every year if we set this kind of precedent."

Mark's mouth dropped. "That's not fair," he whined. "Dad already said I could."

My mom put down her fork. "But it's not just up to your father, Mark. It's a joint decision, and my vote is no."

I shifted in my seat. The weird thing was that I could see both sides of the argument. My mom didn't want to spoil Mark and my dad didn't want to deprive him of something that was so important to him.

"What's the big deal?" my dad replied. "It's not like his bike sits in the garage unused. He rides it every day. And I'm sure we can sell it in the classified ads. I'll take care of it."

"Of course we can sell it. It's practically brand-new," my mom complained. "Any kid would love to have his bike."

My dad started taking very big bites of his lasagna. My mom pushed her plate away.

"What are you going to say next, Hank? That Ellen can get a new bike, too?" my mom asked in a high voice.

"Sure." My dad turned to me. "You want a new bike, too, El?"

"Well, I mean, not if Mom is going to get all upset about it," I said, turning to her.

"I am not upset," she said through gritted teeth.

"Oh, really?" My dad asked, sounding amused. "You look upset."

Red in the face, to be exact.

"I said I'm not upset," she snapped. "What do I care? Get new bikes. For both of them. Get one for yourself while you're at it."

My dad got up from the dinner table and stormed out of the room. My heart started thudding.

"Does this mean I don't get the bike?" Mark asked.

I looked at him in disbelief. "Mark? Get a clue," I said and stormed out of the kitchen myself. Who cared about a stupid bike when World War Three had erupted under our roof?

Five

On Wednesday morning you never would have known my parents had been at each other's throats the night before. My dad leaned back in his chair at the kitchen table, reading the front page of the *Sweet Valley Tribune*. He made this clicking sound with his tongue that he does when he's fascinated by an article. My mom hummed as she flipped pancakes at the stove. She has to be in a pretty good mood to make pancakes on a school day.

Still, I felt something that's sort of hard to explain. Even though they were acting like everything was fine, I was worried a fight might break out any second. I mean, that was happening more and more lately. My parents had become like two boxers in a ring—punching each other, then resting in between rounds.

I think breakfast was a rest period. They were fueling up with food so they could come back in top form for their next round. But the scary thing was that I had no idea when it would begin. I knew there was a chance that it could take place while I was hosting the Unicorn meeting after school. And that was a chance I couldn't take. Especially after I had assured my friends that nothing was wrong with my parents. For the meeting to run smoothly, I would have to make sure that they weren't both at home.

My mom placed a short stack of pancakes in front of me and Mark. When she handed a plate to my dad, he just nodded and took them.

"So," I said, breaking the silence.

My dad looked up from the newspaper. My mom took a seat.

"Remember? I'm hosting the Unicorn meeting after school," I began.

"Again!" Mark complained, his mouth full.

"And I'm just sort of wondering about something," I continued. "Will either of you be here, say, between four and five thirty?"

"Sure will. I'll be putting dinner together," my mom said.

"Daddy?" I asked.

"Let's see." He squinted his eyes, thinking. "Oh, yeah, I have an early day. My last appointment is at three."

Great! Just what I was afraid of. To be safe, I'd have to somehow get rid of one of them.

I turned to my dad. "Isn't there always the chance that someone will need emergency dental care? Isn't it your responsibility as a dentist to be available during daytime hours to keep the teeth of Sweet Valley healthy?"

My dad smiled. "I'm glad to see you're so concerned about the welfare of my patients, but if there's an emergency, my service knows where to find me."

"Well, if you're not busy, you know, maybe you and Mark should go to the bike shop and check out the mountain cruiser," I suggested. "It really would mean a lot to him."

"Yeah!" Mark perked up.

"Mark has piano lessons every Wednesday," my mom said lightly.

Mark pretended to gag.

"Oh," I said slyly. "So you'll probably be picking him up?" I asked my mom.

"Not until after five," she replied.

"But if you're going to be in town, maybe you should swing by the market beforehand and stock up on some . . . canned goods," I urged.

My mom looked at me curiously. "Ellen, I just went to the market yesterday."

"You did?" I asked.

"She did," my dad confirmed.

"But did you remember that creamed corn that I like? Oh, and the baked beans?" I asked.

"Sure did," my mom answered wearily.

My dad put down the paper. "Ellen? Why are you so dead set on getting rid of your folks?"

"Getting rid of you?" I coughed. "Me? No. I just know how loud our meetings can get and I hate to disturb you guys. I mean, I know it must not be easy to be the parents of a teenager." I looked at them sympathetically.

"Oh, Ellen, don't be silly. I adore listening to the chitchat of you and your friends," my mom insisted. "You can host all the meetings you like."

"Well, be warned. We're trying to pick a new president and it could get pretty brutal in there," I said. "We may seem like tame Unicorns, but we turn into wild beasts when we have disagreements."

"Well, maybe I'll whip up a batch of chocolate chip brownies for you and the pack this afternoon," my mom offered, smiling. "Maybe that'll calm you down a little."

"How about if I bring home purple toothbrushes for everyone as a party favor?" my dad suggested.

"Would you?" I asked appreciatively.

They both nodded.

"That'd be excellent," I said.

"What about me?" Mark complained. "What are you going to bring home for me?"

"You want a new toothbrush, you got it," my dad replied.

"I was thinking more like a new baseball mitt," Mark explained.

My dad chuckled and returned to his newspaper, my mom to her humming.

But somehow I still felt nervous. Brownies and toothbrushes were a cool idea, but I just didn't trust my parents anymore. When would the boxers reenter the ring?

When I got home from school that afternoon, my dad was already back from work.

"My three o'clock canceled," he said as he handed over the purple toothbrushes.

"Thanks, Daddy," I said. "These are great."

My mom was letting the brownies cool and offered to write everyone's names on the toothbrush handles with a silver paint pen. She can do these incredibly perfect block letters, and I knew it would be a great touch.

I cut some roses from the garden to put on the table as a centerpiece. After I'd set everything up, I looked around the living room proudly. A tray of gooey brownies, personalized purple toothbrushes, and flowers—the right ingredients for the best meeting ever. And my parents seemed just to be going about their business. It looked like there was nothing to worry about.

But as the clock neared four, I started having my doubts. I was suddenly afraid that at any moment my mom would find some little thing to complain about and send my dad into a total frenzy. My friends would enter the house to the sound of smashing china and crashing appliances.

Thinking fast, I ran to my room, grabbed my portable CD player and my new album, *Johnny Buck: Live From Sweet Valley.*

Back in the living room, I plugged it in and blasted the CD on the highest volume. If my parents started screaming at each other, this would definitely drown them out.

My dad popped into the room. "Isn't that a little loud, El?" he asked, raising his voice.

"I warned you, Daddy." I stepped toward him. "You had the opportunity to stay at the office. We like the music this way. It's meeting procedure."

"What?" my dad said.

"I said I warned you. Sorry," I replied.

My dad shrugged and went back into the kitchen.

I was straightening up the room when Jessica, Lila, and Kimberly appeared. One of my parents must have let them in. I guess the music was so loud that I didn't hear the doorbell ring.

"What's with the music?" Kimberly yelled above the noise.

"You don't like it?" I asked as if this made Kimberly very un-hip.

"Well, I mean, I like it, but I also happen to like being able to hear," she answered.

"We were only outside for, like, ten minutes ringing the doorbell," Lila piped in. "If your dad hadn't come out to do some gardening, we'd still be there."

"Well, sorry, but this CD is so incredible, I just can't stop listening to it. I've already got most of the lyrics down," I bragged. "I thought you guys said you wanted to hear it."

Lila went over to the stereo and switched it off. "Not this loud."

"And we can listen to music later," Jessica suggested. "This is a meeting. We should get down to business."

"Oh. I guess you're right." I sighed.

My stomach was churning. I reminded myself that at least my dad was outside. He could sometimes spend hours working on the garden. Maybe the blaring music wouldn't be necessary, after all.

"So. Welcome to my boardroom," I announced as cheerfully as possible. I signaled my friends over to the table.

Jessica's eyes widened when she saw the spread. "This is really cool, Ellen." She examined a toothbrush.

"These brownies are unbelievable," Lila exclaimed. "My compliments to the chef."

"The roses smell so incredible." Kimberly sniffed a big peach one.

"You can take some home, Kimberly," I offered.

Her face lit up. "Really? My mom will love them. Thanks."

"No problem," I said graciously, starting to get into the swing of things. "Well, I guess this meeting should come to order. The first item on the agenda

is the presidency. Are any of you willing to with-
draw from the race?" I asked, looking at my notes.

Lila, Jessica, and Kimberly looked at me blankly.

"I think we're going to have to do something
creative," I continued. "Like, maybe we could have
a revolving presidency. Like, one month it could be
Lila, another one it could be Jessica."

"*What?*" Lila asked, as if I'd suggested we stop
wearing purple or something.

"That wouldn't work," Kimberly said flatly.

"Maybe we could just draw straws," I suggested.

Jessica shook her head. "Maybe we should just
give it up and talk about Family Day." She giggled.
"My dad got the funniest chef's hat and apron for
barbecuing."

I sighed. It looked as if the presidency topic was
officially over. We'd probably never reach a decision.

"I have to go to the mall on Saturday to pick out
a pair of sandals for my outfit," Lila told us. "Oh,
hey, speaking of the mall, I forgot to tell you my
amazing proposal."

"Really, what?" I didn't really know how everyone else was taking over the meeting, but I had to
admit I was curious about Lila's proposal.

"With the new ice-skating rink, I was thinking
the four of us could form an ice-dancing troupe,"
Lila said excitedly. "My dad offered to rent out the
rink for a party, and we could choreograph a routine and show our stuff."

"That sounds like a blast," Jessica said, beaming.

"Your dad would really do that?" Kimberly asked.

"He's always good on his word," Lila replied with satisfaction. Then she turned to me, looking serious. "So what do you think, Ellen?"

"Oh, it's a great idea," I said quickly. Actually, I wasn't exactly thrilled. I still had a big bruise on my thigh from my fall, and I was a little nervous about getting back on the ice. But expressing doubt when everyone else was so into an idea would definitely not be a cool Unicorn move.

"Of course, you'll need a lot of practice," Jessica told me sternly. "We definitely don't want a repeat of your performance last weekend."

My stomach dropped. Just when I thought my friends were starting to forget all about it, they had to bring up that incredibly embarrassing fall! Why is it always the bad things that people seem to remember?

"Rick Hunter did this hysterical imitation of you in PE, today," Kimberly said, giggling. "He jumped up in the air like a ballerina, dropped to his butt and twisted around, and sprawled out on the pavement like a corpse. You should have seen it, Ellen."

I think it's fair to say I was happy to have missed it. I forced a giggle anyway.

"So you think you can handle it?" Lila asked me.

"Of course I can handle it," I responded, trying to sound cool and confident. "Believe me, it won't happen again. And practice makes perfect. Right?"

"Well, in your case," Kimberly commented, *"anything* will be an improvement."

"Hey, how's your skating outfit doing?" Jessica wondered.

"My outfit?" Did they have to bring up my outfit now?

"It'll definitely need to be fixed before we perform," Lila told me.

"Oh, of course," I said. "Don't worry. I've almost finished."

"Really?" Kimberly sounded impressed. "That's amazing, because it looked way beyond repair."

"Well, it's not. I can hardly wait to wear it again," I told them.

"Good. Let's plan to meet at the rink Sunday after the picnic. It'll be our first rehearsal," Lila suggested. "It will give us an idea about when we'll be ready to perform."

I was feeling queasier by the second. I didn't especially feel like skating in front of my friends, forget performing in front of a whole crowd of people. Not to mention the fact that my skirt looked like a big purple knot. How would I ever pull this off?

"Sounds like a plan," Jessica told Lila, then she turned to me. "Anything else on the agenda?"

I squared my shoulders. "That's it," I said importantly. "This meeting is adjourned."

"So, can I take a few roses?" Kimberly asked just as I heard the front door close. I felt my heart lurch.

My dad was back inside. With all the fuss over the ice troupe business, I'd practically forgotten about my parents. They'd been so quiet all afternoon—which probably meant they were ready for another fight!

I picked the vase off the table. "Just take the whole thing," I told Kimberly. "My mom won't even notice."

Kimberly clutched the vase. "Wow, thanks, Ellen. Are you sure it's OK?"

"Oh, yeah, definitely," I said as I heard my dad walk across the kitchen. "So, I'll see you guys tomorrow."

Lila leaned over and grabbed a brownie for the road. "Do you have something I can wrap this in?"

I picked up the plate. "Take them all. We have tons of leftovers in the kitchen."

"Really?" Lila asked.

I could hear the murmur of my parents conversation. I began to feel shaky.

"Yes!" I gasped.

"Hey. What about listening to the album?" Jessica mentioned.

"Another time," I said, pushing them toward the doorway.

"Oh, come on, Ellen," she protested. "I want to hear it."

"You want to hear it? Take it." I dashed over to the CD and put it in its case. "Don't worry about returning it."

Jessica gave me a weird look. "Well, OK. Thanks."

"I'll see you guys." I opened the door and practically shoved them onto the stoop.

Lila turned back to me. "Is everything OK, Ellen?"

"Everything's great." I forced a huge smile and closed the door in their faces.

Six

Dinner was pretty much a repeat performance of breakfast, except that we had hamburgers instead of pancakes. My mom hummed every time she got up from the table and my dad made the clicking noise with his tongue even though he wasn't reading the newspaper.

I was glad that everyone was pretty much in their own world, since I wanted to mull over the Unicorn meeting that afternoon. Overall, it had been a supreme success. The toothbrushes, the brownies, and the flowers had all scored major points in the hostess-with-the-mostess department. Kimberly had called as soon as she got home to tell me how much her mother loved the bouquet of roses.

But somehow I was still a little bummed out. How long were my friends going to pick on me for falling on the ice? You'd think teasing me was their absolute favorite activity. I mean, if by some bizarre circumstance, say, Jessica had wiped out, I doubt they'd pick on her for the rest of her life. And you can imagine that being in an ice troupe was the last thing in the world I was prepared to do. (By the way, what *is* an ice troupe, anyway?)

But there was no getting out of it. I had pretended to be excited and now I had to go along with it.

And somehow I'd have to save that disaster of a skating outfit, or else I'd *never* hear the end of it.

Yep, it's an absolute, total disaster, I thought glumly as I fished out my skirt from my dresser after dinner.

To begin with, I would have to remove the stitches I had put in the other night.

I snipped the end of the thread and carefully pulled on the royal-blue string. But it got stuck in the fabric. I tugged and yanked and weaseled it around with my fingers. Eventually I got the thread out. I also wound up with snags running horizontally throughout the skirt.

Tears sprang to my eyes. Every time I had tried to make it look better, I made it look worse. Even Lila's father's tailor couldn't have turned it back into what it once was—the prettiest skating costume that I had ever seen.

I buried my face in my hands. It had been so

generous of my parents to give me the beautiful skirt. I had gleamed when I opened the box and saw the lavender chiffon underneath the tissue paper. I had counted down the days till I could wear it. But now, for the first time, I had to admit that it didn't have a chance of survival. I had pulled a typical Ellen. I had messed up something that meant a lot to me.

Suddenly I heard voices erupt from downstairs. I tossed the skirt (if you could even call it that) aside and dashed out to the hallway to listen. *Probably just another false alarm,* I told myself.

"Calm down, Hank!" my mom pleaded.

I stepped back, startled by her high pitch.

"I don't want to hear it anymore," my dad hollered.

I noticed that Mark was leaning out the door of his room, too. He looked frightened.

"Where are my keys, Nancy!"

"Don't leave. Don't leave until we resolve this," my mom cried.

"We'll never resolve it!"

"Hank, come back here. I'm warning you. Come back here."

I heard the front door slam. My heart froze. Mark ran back into his room. I did the same. I guess neither of us wanted my mom to know that we had overheard them.

But what was it that we had overheard? What did it all mean?

I sat back down on my bed in a daze, trying to make some sense of what was happening. At least I was old enough to know that husbands and wives fight. It was a normal part of marriage. So why was I letting myself get so worried? My parents were probably just going through a phase. Like Mark was in that pesty phase. And I was in that ditsy phase. They just happened to be in that snappy, biting, fighting, screaming, hollering, crazy kind of phase. Everything was going to be OK. My dad would come back with flowers and a box of chocolates, apologize for leaving in a huff, and plan a family vacation to Hawaii for all of us.

There was a knock on my door. "Ellen?" my mother called out.

My chest tightened as I realized that the lavender blob was sitting on my bed in plain sight. No parent was coming into this room until I got rid of the evidence.

"Just a sec, Mom," I said as I stuffed the skirt underneath a pillow. I picked up my English book and leaned against my bedpost, trying to look like someone in the middle of a serious study session. I was not about to let on that I had been eavesdropping either. "OK, you can come in."

My mom stepped inside. She looked terrible. Red eyes and pale skin.

I clutched the book in my arms. "What's up, Mom?"

My mom just looked at me, her lips pursed.

"I'm sort of finishing a chapter, here," I told her.
"So if you don't have anything to say, I should
probably get back to work so I can go to bed."

But instead of turning around, my mom sat
down on the bed next to me, dangerously near the
pillow that hid my skirt. "Look, Ellen, I think we
should talk."

"Do we have to?" I asked feebly. "I'm tired and I
still have some homework to do. Can't it wait till
the morning?"

"I just thought maybe we could . . ." my mom
stuttered. She looked around at the stuff on my
bed. She ran her fingers over the silky edge of my
woolen blanket. Her hand brushed against the in-
criminating pillow.

I awkwardly rearranged my body so that I was
on top of it. "What, Mom?" I pressed.

"I just want you to know that you can ask me
anything," she said as she picked up my teddy bear
and retied the bow around his neck.

"That's nice to know, Mom, but now's not the
time. Do you mind?" I took Teddy back and
opened the book to a random page, pretending to
read.

My mom sat there, looking down at the bed-
spread.

"I'm trying to improve my grades this semes-
ter," I went on. "I really have to get back to work."
I hated to waste a good line, but it was a do-or-die
situation.

Finally my mom got up and brushed the bangs off my forehead. "Good night, Ellen." She sighed quietly before she slipped out and closed the door.

That night, I tossed and turned under my covers, listening for the sound of my dad's car pulling into the driveway or his keys in the door. But the hours passed on my digital clock, and still he didn't come home.

What was going on with my parents? My dad had never left the house that way. There was so much anger in his voice, he didn't even sound like himself.

I gazed across the room at an old blown-up photograph of me and my parents, illuminated by my night-light. I'm in the middle, my dad is making bunny ears behind my head, and my mom is pinching my cheek with her fingers. I stared at the picture longingly. Why couldn't I just rewind to Family Day last year when my mom and dad weren't so angry with each other? When we were like a normal, happy family? When my parents giggled together and took first place in the three-legged race? Would they ever be that way again?

Seven

"Taco salad," my mom said in a singsong voice the next night at dinner. Her eyes were twinkling as she placed a yellow ceramic bowl in the center of the table.

"Yum!" I exclaimed, spreading my napkin over my lap. "Taco salad is my favorite."

I couldn't believe I'd been so upset last night. Everything seemed back to normal. My dad was back from wherever he had gone. (The office to catch up on some paperwork, maybe? People in the nineties are known for working odd hours, right?) My mom looked radiant in a red sweater and her anniversary pearls.

I took a large portion of salad and sprinkled some extra grated cheese on top. "Here, Daddy," I said, passing the container his way.

My dad took it and put it down. I noticed that neither of my parents had served themselves. *More for me*, I thought.

"Well. You won't believe what's going on with the Unicorns," I said in between bites. "Maybe you guys can give me some advice. See, we need a new president, and it's, like, Jessica, Lila, and Kimberly are all dead set on it being them. But no one will give it up. And they'd each be great in a different way. So how on earth are we supposed to chose?"

My dad stared at his glass of water. My mom looked at me. "Ellen, maybe now's not the time to talk about this," she said gently.

I frowned. "Why?"

"It's never the time to talk about your ugly friends." Mark made a face at me.

"Mark," my mom said warningly.

"Let's talk about going to the racetrack," Mark said. "Jim and his dad went, and they, like, won—"

"Mark," my mom broke in. "Not now, honey."

My dad pushed his chair away from the table. "Ellen. Mark. Your mother and I have something to tell you."

I tried to hold back my smile. My dad had this serious look on his face that he makes when he's trying to hide a surprise from us.

"Oh," I said slyly. "Do tell."

Maybe it was the Hawaiian vacation that I had thought about last night. Or a backyard swimming pool or the puppy Mark and I had been begging for. It would be his special way of apologizing for all the fighting we had been subjected to.

I leaned forward anxiously. My dad turned to my mom.

"Your mother and I are getting a divorce," he said.

I felt the blood rush from my face. "What?"

"Honey, I think you heard him. We're getting a divorce," my mom said softly.

My stomach dropped. "But why!" My words came out in a screech.

"Ellen, it should be no mystery to you that we haven't been getting along," my mom explained.

"Well, my friends and I don't always get along either. But do we break up? No! We talk and work out our differences." Well, sort of, but it was not the time to get into a detailed analysis of how half the Unicorns had become Angels.

"This is a little more complicated than a friendship, honey," my dad said, trying to calm me down. "We will try to help you understand it as best we can."

I threw down my napkin. "Oh, I understand it all right. You guys are just giving it up because of a few lousy fights."

"It's not a few lousy fights, Ellen. We've been on the rocks for years," my dad said quietly.

"But if you have to, why can't you just have, like, a trial separation?" I suggested desperately. "People do that all the time, and they get back together because they realize how much they love each other."

My parents stared at me in silence. Even Mark was quiet, staring at my parents in total bewilderment.

Finally my dad crossed his arms over his chest. "For a long time we've been trying to get it together. For the sake of you two."

"But it isn't working," my mom added weakly. "We're miserable the way it is. And we've realized that it's more damaging to you to hear us battle it out day and night."

"I'd rather hear you fight than have you get a divorce," I screamed.

"Ellen, calm down," my mom pleaded.

"No!" I yelled. "Go ahead and fight. Scream. Yell at each other. Have I ever complained? Once? I didn't even say anything to you the other day when my friends all heard you having it out."

"Your friends heard us?" My mom looked ashamed. "Oh, Ellen."

"But they knew it wasn't a big deal, because their parents fight, too. Everybody fights. I mean, I fight with Mark, and do you see me filing for a new brother?"

"The hardest part about this decision was our concern about how it would affect you," my dad said.

"Then why are you doing this to us? Why?" I demanded.

My dad looked down. "Because we can't go on this way. I've signed a lease for an apartment downtown. It's close to both of your schools, so the two of you will be able to come by in the afternoons and spend the weekends with me."

Mark looked stunned. "You mean you're not going to live here anymore?"

My mom put her hand on Mark's shoulder. "That's what people do when they get a divorce, honey."

Mark pushed her hand away. "I want to live with you, Dad. I can't be the only boy here," he cried. "Please don't leave."

My mom buried her face in her hands.

"You'll be the man of the house, Mark. You have to stay to take care of your mother and your sister," my dad told him.

"I don't want to be," he cried. "I'll run away. I will."

"You'll get used to it, Mark," my mom tried to assure him.

"I know this is all very sudden, but I'm packing my things up and leaving tonight," my dad said. "There's no sense in dragging this out."

"Tonight?" I shrieked.

"I know it's hard to understand, but it will be better this way. You'll see," my mom said gently.

I couldn't believe this was happening. It was just too much, too soon. My parents were actually getting a divorce. When I sat down for dinner I was a

part of a four-member family. I hadn't even made a
dent in my salad and I was now part of a broken
home. A broken home—when Family Day was just
a few days away.

"What about the picnic?" I blurted out.

They both looked puzzled.

"What picnic, Ellen?" my dad asked patiently.

"Family Day!" I cried with frustration.
"Remember? Mom and I are going to make fried
chicken and biscuits. Don't you remember how
much fun we all had last year? You guys won the
three-legged race."

"Your mother will be going," my dad said at the
exact same time that my mom said, "Your father
will be going."

"Why can't you both go? Why can't you post-
pone your stupid divorce and do something that's
important to me?"

My mom leaned toward me. "We'll figure something out, Ellen. Don't worry about it."

"Don't worry about it? Is that all you can say?"
My throat was sore from yelling, but I didn't care.
"How could you do this to me? I will never forgive
either of you."

I pushed back my chair and stormed out of the
kitchen.

I threw myself on my bed, tears rolling down
my cheeks. Burying my head in a pillow, I cried
and cried until I realized it was the pillow I had

hidden my skating skirt underneath the night before. Without thinking about what I was doing, I grabbed the outfit from underneath the pillow and pulled with all my might. In an instant I had torn it in half.

There, I thought, feeling triumphant for a moment. Then I threw the scraps to the ground, crying even harder.

How could I have been so stupid? I thought. Any normal kid would have seen the signs. The constant bickering and arguing, my dad's storming out of the house. . . . If I'd had any sort of a brain I could have prepared myself for the inevitable.

I stared at the lavender scraps on the ground, feeling totally alone. Should I call Lila or Jessica or Kimberly? I wondered. Maybe talking to them would make me feel better, I thought, reaching for the phone.

Then I stopped. Whom was I kidding? This wasn't something they could ever understand. Sure, Lila's parents were divorced, but that was different. It happened forever ago when Lila was a little girl. She was too young to understand, and it was probably easy for her to adjust to the change. And now she and her dad had a wonderful life together, complete with charge cards and vacations and catered picnics. And Jessica's and Kimberly's families were as perfect as families in those TV sitcoms from the fifties.

Besides, this would just give them something

else to tease me about. After they overheard my parents' argument, they were so freaked out they didn't even want me hosting a meeting. And that was after just one argument. I could only imagine how they'd react to the idea of divorce.

A million horrible thoughts rushed through my head. What if they looked down on me, or blamed me for what had happened? What if they decided that a girl with such a messy family wasn't Unicorn material? I could forget about hosting another meeting, that was for sure. In fact, maybe they'd even boot me from the club. I would be left with nothing at all.

No matter what, I decided, the Unicorns would never find out.

Eight

"So my mom got this bread machine," Jessica said the next day at lunch as she opened her carton of milk. "You just pour in the dough and a perfectly shaped loaf comes out. We're going to bring some to . . ."

Don't say it. Please, don't say it!

". . . Family Day."

I felt sick every time I heard those words.

"Well, my father and I are having a professional photographer come," Lila said, tucking her hair behind her ear. "We haven't had a nice shot of the two of us in a while. He likes to have one in his office to put on his desk."

I bit my lip, doing my best not to cry. It was Friday, and Family Day was only two days away. It seemed that it was all anyone could talk about.

"The lake and the trees will make a totally gorgeous background," Lila went on.

"Just be sure you don't wear your hat. Hats in pictures never work," Jessica told her authoritatively.

"Oh, no, I wouldn't want to cover my hair," Lila said, looking horrified. "I'm going to curl the ends of my hair and wear some light pink lipstick." She sucked in her cheeks.

"Do you think the photographer will take one picture of the four of us?" Kimberly asked.

"That would be so cool to have a blowup of the Unicorns," Jessica said excitedly. "We could get purple frames and put Unicorn decals all over them."

I looked down at my tuna sandwich. Normally, I'd be really into that idea, but I couldn't imagine being able to muster up a smile when the photographer said "Cheese."

"Well, he gets paid by the hour, so I'll have to ask," Lila replied. "But you know my dad. He'll pretty much do anything for me."

"The picnic is going to be amazing this year." Jessica looked dreamy. "I heard that there are going to be a lot more games, an obstacle course, face painting, and this machine that they rented where you aim for the bull's-eye and try and dunk your dad."

"Or your mom," Kimberly added.

"I'm personally after my dad." Jessica raised her eyebrows. "I've been begging for an allowance increase forever. He won't budge."

"Who are you after, Ellen?" Kimberly asked.

"Me?" I coughed.

"Is there anyone else here that goes by Ellen?" Kimberly teased. "Of course you, dummy."

I shifted uncomfortably in my seat.

"So who's it going to be? Your dad or your mom?" Jessica wondered.

"Oh, well, I'm not sure yet," I stammered.

There was no doubt about it—I was in a terrible bind. I was dead set on not letting the Unicorns find out the truth about the divorce. But on Sunday, how would I ever explain to them one parent's absence? If I brought my mom, I guess I could tell them that, devoted dentist that he was, my dad had to do an emergency root canal. He was disappointed, but duty called. Or, I could bring my dad and tell them my mom was in bed with an awful bug. I'd say that my dad offered to stay home and take care of her like a loving, caring husband. But being the generous, kind woman that she is, she insisted that we go ahead without her. Hearing all about our adventures would be almost as good as being there.

"I'd like to nail your dad," Jessica said enthusiastically.

My mouth dropped. Did she know something that she wasn't supposed to? I clutched the table. "Why?"

"I want to get him back for all that torture in the dentist's chair." She giggled.

I sighed. "Oh. That's funny." I tried to smile, to show how funny it was.

"Do you guys want to hear something totally embarrassing?" Kimberly asked. "My mom had these ridiculous shirts made up that say 'I'm Kimberly's Mom,' 'I'm Kimberly's Dad' and 'These Are My Lucky Parents.' Like I'm really going to embarrass myself in front of the entire school and show up at the picnic in that. If they force me to wear it, I'm planning to sink them both in the dunk tank." She cracked her knuckles.

"Parents can be such a pain," Jessica sighed. "My mom said I had to clean out underneath my bed. Like, why should she care? It's my bed, not hers."

"Please. My dad nearly had a heart attack because I accidentally left a soda can on his antique mahogany table and it made a water ring." Lila rolled her eyes. "I mean, isn't that what keeps furniture refinishers in business?"

I looked at my friends in disbelief. I wanted to scream, "What nerve do you have to put down your parents? At least they're going out of their way to make Family Day special for you."

But I couldn't risk blowing my cover by getting angry. One slip and they'd know something was up. My friends were pretty good detectives, after all.

In fact, they'd probably suspect something was fishy if I went for the old root canal excuse. I would have to be more sneaky. Hmm. . . . What would

Jessica do in this kind of situation? She would see the picnic as an opportunity. A way to patch things up with her parents! Maybe, just maybe, there was a way to get them both to show up after all. And with both parents there, I wouldn't have to explain a thing to my friends.

I tapped my finger against the table, thinking. Then suddenly it came to me. I could tell my dad that I wanted him to be my guest, and then tell my mom the same. I would ask them both to meet me at the picnic because as a civic-minded student, I had agreed to arrive early to help the organizing committee set up some of the games.

My parents would both show up, not expecting a thing. But as soon as they laid eyes on each other at the beautiful, romantic lake setting and saw how all the other families were having such a great time, they would realize how silly and stubborn they'd been. They'd see that they belonged together. During a private canoe ride on the lake, my dad would serenade my mom. They would share a wild kiss, apologize for behaving so ridiculously, and live happily ever after. It would be like a scene from a great movie.

Years from now my parents would toast me at their fiftieth wedding anniversary. They would tell their guests that though it was hard to believe, they had once considered a divorce. However, thanks to their clever daughter and a charming little plot of hers, they had been forced to see the light.

And my friends? They would be none the wiser, and my status as a Unicorn would be intact.

"Hello? Anybody in there?" Jessica was tapping on my forehead with her fist.

I looked up at her. "Why? What?"

"You've been, like, zoning out all lunch," Lila told me.

"Me?" I asked. "I have not!"

"Then what have we been talking about for the last ten minutes?" Kimberly challenged.

"The picnic," I replied firmly.

Lila rolled her eyes. "Come back down to earth, Ellen, we talked about the picnic for about a second. We've been discussing the ice troupe the whole time."

"Oh, right." Another dreaded subject. "I meant *first* we talked Family Day and then we talked ice troupe."

Jessica raised her eyebrow skeptically. "Sometimes I don't know how you get through the day in one piece. You are just so out there."

And I guess I could see her point. I was doing a lot of spacing out lately. But once I managed to get my parents back together, I'd laugh at anyone who dared call me an airhead. Only a mastermind could pull off such a feat.

There was no time to waste. I began to lay the groundwork for my plot the second the last bell rang at school. Instead of going to Casey's with my friends, I walked directly to my dad's dental office on the other side of town. He worked in a tall glass building in the business district, where a lot of other doctors had their practices.

The elevator let me off on the third floor and I marched right over to the receptionist, Louise.

"Ellen!" she exclaimed when she saw me. "Is your dad expecting you?"

I leaned up against the glass window. "Not exactly, Louise, but if you could tell him I need to talk to him for a second, that would be great."

She gave me a friendly nod and I sat down in the waiting room, nervously jiggling my knees. This just *had* to work. It had to!

"El?" my dad said, leaning out the entry door. He was in his white dentist's smock. "You can come back."

I followed him into his small office down the hall.

"I'm just waiting for Bruce Patman to get his fluoride treatment so I can check him for cavities," he said as he sat down behind his desk.

"Bruce Patman gets fluoride treatments?" I was stunned.

Bruce seemed so perfect that I didn't think he'd need to worry about things like getting fillings. It was weird to get this inside information.

"Every kid gets a fluoride treatment when they come to see me." My dad laughed wickedly.

"So who has the most cavities?" I asked.

My dad grinned. "Well, that's confidential," he teased.

"Oh." I sighed.

My dad shifted in his seat. "Look, Ellen, I'm glad you came by."

I nodded. "I just wanted to tell you in person that I was sorry about acting like a total baby last night."

After all, the last my dad had seen me I had gone shrieking out of the kitchen. He'd knocked on my door, but I wouldn't let him come in to say good-bye.

"No, no, Ellen. Don't apologize. There's no easy way to break that kind of news. Or take it." He looked across the desk at me, his eyes welling up with tears. "There's no one in the world I care about more than you and Mark. I'd never want to hurt you."

"I know dad, I know." I fixed him with my most mature look. "Listen, I don't want to keep Bruce waiting, but I came here to invite you to come to Family Day with me."

My dad raised his eyebrows. "Are you sure your mother—"

"Oh, I talked to mom this morning," I said quickly. "She agreed that it would only be fair for you to come, since you and I will only be spending time together on the weekends from now on."

He lit up. "Oh, Ellen, I'm thrilled. I would love to be your guest."

Well, that was easy. I think it would be fair to say that I had more promise as a schemer than as a seamstress.

"Then it's settled." I got up from my seat. "Of course, the two of us will have to prepare a picnic, but how hard could that be?"

"I think it's in the realm of my talents," my dad said, smiling.

"So do I," I agreed.

My dad looked at me fondly. "I think we could really use the time together. Maybe I can try to explain why we decided to get a divorce."

"No need to explain, Daddy," I said with a confident smile. And I meant it. He'd be planning his second honeymoon by the time Family Day was over.

FDRPPP2 (Family Day Reunion Plot Preparation Part Two. I'm a schemer, so from now on, everything will be in code) was just as easy to set up as the first. I was waiting in the kitchen reading the latest issue of *Teen Talk* when my mom came in with Mark.

"Ellen," she said in a surprised tone. "I thought you'd be with the Unicorns at Casey's."

Mark grabbed a couple graham crackers from the cookie jar and ran upstairs.

"Nope. I had to stop by and see Dad instead." I put down the magazine.

"Oh," she said softly.

"Listen, Mom, I'm really, really sorry I acted that way this morning." At breakfast I'd told my mom I would never speak to her again. I said that anyone who would get a divorce and ruin her daughter's life was not even worthy of being a mother. "I don't want to make this any harder on you."

My mom joined me at the table. "Well, I could use your support, Ellen."

"Well, you have it. And anyway, in case you're wondering, the reason I went to see Dad was to talk to him about Family Day."

My mom exhaled and looked down.

"He said it was OK if I took you instead of him. I mean, he wanted to go, but I explained that I wouldn't be able to spend weekends with you anymore." I looked at her expectantly. "So what do you say?"

"Oh, Ellen, I'd love to go," my mom replied. "I really think we could use a day to just be together as mother and daughter."

I smiled. My mom was as easily duped as my dad.

Obviously, FDRP was going to be a huge success.

My mom reached for my hand. "I know that the divorce is going to be hard on you, Ellen. And I'm glad that you have such a close group of friends to turn to, but I want you to be able to talk about it with me, too."

"Let's not worry about it, and talk about the picnic instead." I reached for my mom's recipe box and handed it to her. "Now let's go over that menu. I want to make it a perfect day."

Nine

As we'd planned, I met the rest of the Unicorns at the Valley Mall on Saturday morning. Lila had to pick up a pair of sandals for her outfit. Kimberly was looking for new jeans (a bribe from her mom to get her to wear the "These Are My Lucky Parents" T-shirt). Jessica was shopping for a lavender headband to replace the one she had lost somewhere in between her bedroom and school.

And me? Label it FDRPPP3. My mission was to add some romantic atmosphere to the picnic spread.

"Sheesh, you'd think the printing could at least have been in purple." Kimberly was still going on about the Family Day T-shirt. "What were they thinking?"

"Who knows?" Jessica said with a flip of her

hair. "My mom was so annoyed that I lost another headband. You'd think I lost a priceless jewel by the way she yelled at me."

"Well, I really can't believe my dad put up a fight about my sandals," Lila complained. "He actually had the nerve to ask me if there was something in my closet that I could use."

"I guess it's my turn to complain about my parents," I piped in.

They all turned to me.

"They gave me a list of all this stuff they want to make the picnic extra special." I pulled a sheet from the pocket of my jean shorts. "A pink picnic blanket, wineglasses, candles, and some handmade chocolate hearts from The Chocoholic." On my walk to the mall I had stopped by the bank and withdrawn my life savings to cover these luxurious but critical expenses. The way I saw it, I was investing in my future.

"Your parents really want that?" Jessica asked curiously.

Yep, they do, I said to myself. *They just don't know it yet.*

"Ellen?" Jessica pressed.

"Well, why wouldn't they?" I asked.

Jessica shrugged. "I don't know. It just sounds like the kind of stuff you would use for a romantic dinner, not a family picnic on the lake."

I smiled. *A romantic dinner.* That was exactly the image I'd wanted.

"And, I mean, candles during the *day*?" Lila asked. "That sounds like one of *your* stupid ideas, not your parents'."

I put my hands on my hips. "Well, the spark never dies with my mom and dad."

"Whatever you say." Kimberly held up her palms and shrugged.

"I guess you're getting plastic wineglasses," Lila said, "or didn't you think of that?"

"Oh, plastic, right. So they don't break? I think that's what my mom requested," I muttered, pretending to double-check the list. "There it is. *Plastic wineglasses.*"

"Anyway, I say we hit the shoe store first," Lila suggested.

"I'd rather pick out my headband," Jessica said.

"Well, what about my jeans? It always takes a while to find just the right ones," Kimberly chimed in.

"I've got a lot on my checklist, you guys," I pointed out. "How about coming with me to one of my stops first?"

Kimberly sighed. "Why don't we just meet in the food court in an hour? That way we can all take care of our errands and still have time to eat lunch and scope out the scene. I heard that Aaron, Peter, and Bruce are going to be here."

"Say no more," Lila said, applying a fresh coat of lipstick.

"Food court. Twelve forty-five," Jessica confirmed, checking her watch.

With that, the four of us went our separate ways.

As I rounded the corner, I picked up speed. It was time for some major romantic scheming.

My first stop was the Candle Wick, which boasts the biggest selection of candles in all of Sweet Valley. They stock every color, scent, size, and shape that you could ever dream of. Floating gardenia candles. Peppermint-scented sticks shaped like big candy canes. Round balls that look like miniature stained-glass windows. You could almost taste the incredible mix of smells that fills up the store.

I went up and down the rows, admiring everything. But I couldn't decide on what to buy. Choosing one kind from a million possibilities was more complicated than picking out a party dress (which was no easy task).

"Looks like you could use some help," a raspy voice called out.

I put down the vanilla votive candle that I was sniffing and looked up. A tall pregnant woman stood before me. A checkered dress clung to her belly and her hair was pulled back in a long braid.

"You work here?" I asked.

"Until I start going into contractions," she joked. "Then my manager will take over."

"By the time I decide what to buy, you probably will have delivered," I said.

"You're torn?" she asked.

I nodded. "Yes. I want *everything*."

"Well, it's easy to narrow down if you follow my simple guidelines. Do you want something decorative, freestanding, for a candelabra, or for candlesticks? Would you prefer scented or unscented? Is it a gift or for yourself, and do you have a price limit?" She smiled.

"Actually, it's for my parents. They haven't been getting along too well," I confessed. "I'm trying to set . . . a mood."

"Oh," she replied knowingly.

"The candles have got to be hard-core romantic. And I'm prepared to splurge." I patted on my purse.

"That won't be necessary," she told me. "Follow me."

We went to the other side of the store, passing a candle shaped like a triple scoop of ice cream. I would remember it when it came time to buy Jessica a birthday gift. But for now I had to keep my focus.

"Well, it's your lucky day. Romance is my area of expertise," the woman told me.

"Well, that's good, because a lot is at stake here."

"About five years ago I had a boyfriend named Billy," the woman went on. "I was on the fence about him. I couldn't decide if he was going to be 'the one.'"

I didn't know where she was going with this, but I listened intently.

"Well, he invited me over for dinner at his apartment. Let's see." She paused for a second. "He burned the chicken, undercooked the baked potatoes, got the wine cork stuck in the bottle, and dropped the cake on the floor. But."

"But?" I asked with wide eyes.

"He had these cinnamon-burgundy candles scattered all over the room." She picked up a cinnamon-burgundy votive from the display.

I widened my eyes. "Did his apartment burn down?"

"Not exactly." She clutched the candles and beamed.

"So what happened?" The suspense was killing me.

"I married him." She rubbed her hand over her stomach. "I mean, that wasn't the evening that he proposed. But when I think back to that night, I don't so much remember the disaster as I do those incredible candles. The spicy scent, the rich color. They just set the mood. It was the first night I realized that I was in love with Billy."

She held out a candle to me and I inhaled its fragrant scent. It was exotic and mystical and intoxicating.

"The smell just brings me back," she said dreamily, taking a whiff. "I opened this store so I could spread the word."

I turned to my adviser and I said what any

girl would have in a similar situation. "Sold."

At the candy store, the routine was pretty much the same. I asked for a half pound of chocolate hearts to bring love back to a fading marriage. The lady behind the counter had a thick Southern accent, bleached blond hair, and an enormous diamond on her ring finger.

"You've got it all wrong, darlin'," she said, after I had briefed her on my predicament. "I've got an honorary degree in marriage counseling, so I know about these things. Those hearts are a little too cutesy-wootsy. I'd go with something more sensual." She leaned forward, ready to divulge her wisdom.

"Please. Suggest," I encouraged her.

"A block of choc-o-late. The lovers can nibble-nibble on it at the same time."

"Oh. I get it," I said, smiling. "It's like a love potion."

"Works every time," she said, wiggling her eyebrows. "And take it from me. I've gotten married to the same gentleman three times."

What more proof did I need? "It's settled," I told her. "I'll take one extra-small block of milk chocolate."

"That's the right idea, doll," she said, and selected one from the case.

"I'm a fast learner," I said confidently.

She examined the chocolate block in her palm as

if it were a precious gem. "Yup. This'll do the job."

She rang it up at the cash register.

"Satisfaction guaranteed or your money back," she promised as she handed me my change.

"Far as I'm concerned, this is a final sale," I replied.

When I got home, I rushed past my mom, who was reading a cookbook at the kitchen table.

"Hi! Bye!" I couldn't take a chance of her seeing my bundle of supplies.

"Mmmm," she replied, not looking up from the book. "Hi."

I dashed up the stairs two at a time. I was in the best mood I'd been in all week long. I had been just as successful in the other stores. At the linen shop I bought a gorgeous pale pink blanket that thankfully was on sale. And I tracked down plastic wineglasses in the housewares section of a department store. And I hadn't even taken a bite from the chunk of chocolate on my walk back home. Talk about willpower.

I locked my door behind me and pulled everything out of the bags. I had to do a practice setup. I laid out the blanket on my carpet. Pieces of paper served as plates. I put them very close to each other and used pencils for the utensils. The glasses were so pretty, they didn't even look plastic. I was planning to sneak a bottle of wine my parents had gotten as a Christmas present and had been saving for a special occasion, which clearly hadn't come till now. It would go on the edge of the blanket—I set down a shampoo bottle to mark the exact place. I spread the candles all over the blanket and put the chocolate on a little dish in the middle.

I stepped back and tilted my head, like an artist examining her creation. But something was missing.

I frowned. I really could have used the advice of someone with some design savvy like Lila. But as you know, this was not an option. Instead, I would just have to trust myself to think like her. *What belongs at a romantic picnic for two? What would Lila bring?* I asked myself. Wine, chocolate, candles . . . flowers! The perfect touch would be fresh flowers scattered all over the blanket. I could pick them from our flower garden in the morning.

And where would I sit during the reunion? I'd probably be so jittery that I wouldn't be able to eat a thing. And for the real effect, I knew my mom and dad had to be left alone. I would hang out with the Wakefields or with Lila and her father while my parents rekindled the flame.

I carefully folded the blanket and hid everything under my bed before I went back downstairs to hang out with my mom.

"I'm in the mood to cook up a storm," my mom said when I walked back into the kitchen. A bunch of cookbooks were stacked on the kitchen table. "Mark talked me into letting him play with Jim on Sunday, so we don't have to be bogged down with his prerequisite peanut butter-and-jelly sandwich and apple with the skin peeled off."

"Cool!" I was glad to know that Mark wouldn't be there to get in the way of anything.

"You know, I think that cooking for the picnic is just what I need," she added. "I've really been down in the dumps. But baking, in particular, has an incredible therapeutic effect on me."

Funny, licking the batter always has a way of cheering me up when I'm down. "So let's make dessert first," I suggested.

"I thought you'd never ask." She smiled. "I've narrowed it down. I'm thinking we go traditional and make giant chocolate chip cookies. Or we go fancy and make individual fruit tarts. Or we go all out and make a strawberry shortcake."

Wasn't the answer obvious? My dad drooled over the strawberry shortcake that my mom had made for his birthday one year. "I'm thinking the cake," I told her.

I sighed happily. One bite out of the cake and memories of the good times would come rushing back to my dad. He would reminisce for a while and then tell my mom that the cake was so delicious she should consider opening her own bakery in Sweet Valley. "It would be a gold mine, darling," he would say fondly. And my mom, who's always a sucker for a compliment, would giggle like a teenager. "You really think I'm *that* talented, Hank?" she would ask flirtatiously as my dad kissed her on the neck.

"Yes, strawberry shortcake will definitely do the job," I added as I slipped into an apron. "Just tell me what to do."

Ten

My hand shook as I pushed 409 on the call box outside my dad's apartment complex. It was Sunday. Family Day. D-day. FDRP day. Call it what you want, but to me it was plain and simple. It was the day to reinstate the Ritemans as a family of four. Needless to say, I was a nervous wreck.

"El? Is that you?" My dad's voice came through the speaker on the call box.

"It's me," I confirmed.

"I'm going to buzz you in. Take the elevator up to the fourth floor, turn left, and I'll be waiting outside my unit. OK?"

"In. Up. Fourth floor. Left." I exhaled. "Got it."

Buzzzzzz.

I reached for the handle, but my jittery hand slipped as the buzz stopped.

Frustrated, I pushed #409 again.

"Daddy," I said after he had answered. "Can we try that one more time?"

Buzzzzzz.

This time I lunged for the handle and made it inside.

It looked like an OK place. There were big beige sofas and glass coffee tables in the lobby area. Huge prints of waves crashing on the shore hung along the walls. The carpeting was cream-colored with squares of brown, blue, and beige. It felt more like a hotel than a place to live, but who cared? This was only a temporary arrangement as far as I was concerned.

The elevator dropped me off on the fourth floor. I took a few deep breaths as I walked down the long hallway. If my dad detected my nervous energy, he might guess something was up.

As promised, my dad was waiting outside his apartment. I was so happy to see him that I automatically loosened up. He was still in his pajamas and the big blue terry-cloth robe that Mark and I gave him last Christmas. I gave him a hug.

"I have a key for you so you won't have to go through that crazy beeper thing again," my dad said as he kissed me on the forehead.

He was unshaven and his face felt sort of sandpapery.

"Don't you shave anymore?" I asked as I pulled away.

He rubbed his hand over his jawline. "I've

had this sudden urge to grow a beard."

"Dad. That's gross. That's totally not you."

"Oh, but it is," my dad argued. "I always talked about growing a beard, and your mother objected every time."

I frowned. Obviously, a beard wouldn't go over too well with my mom at the picnic.

"But what will your patients say?" I asked.

My dad rumpled my hair. "There's no law against growing a beard. You'll get used to it."

"But—Mark won't even recognize you," I tried again. "You'll frighten him."

"Ellen, he's ten," my dad said patiently. "And I don't tell you to cut your hair because I think it would look nicer if it were shorter."

I rolled my eyes. "Oh-kay."

"Now, do you want to come in and see my new pad or are we going to hang out in the hallway all morning?"

I shrugged. "Why not?"

He took my hand and we stepped inside.

"Well?" he asked. "What do you think?" He flung out his arm like a game-show hostess.

My mouth dropped. It wasn't even a home. It was a big open space with nothing in it. A box.

"I've got a view of downtown from the living room, and the window back here overlooks the courtyard area. There's a pool, Jacuzzi, tennis courts, and a weight room that I will be putting to use." He flexed his biceps.

"But, Dad," I protested. "It's . . ."

"Empty?" he filled in.

"Right." That is, except for the hideous chrome chandelier dangling from the ceiling.

"I was hoping I could coax you into coming furniture shopping with me next weekend," he said. "Provided that you don't try to talk me into buying a purple couch and lavender throw pillows."

I had to stifle my grin. Playing interior decorator would be fun and everything, but by next weekend my dad would be happily living back at home. "Nothing in the purple family," I assured him, so I wouldn't arouse his suspicions. "I promise."

"This place is only a two-bedroom, so when you and Mark come together, one of us will have to sleep in the living room," my dad said. "I think we'll have to get one of those hide-a-bed things, and I was thinking we'd pick out a big-screen TV to put in the corner here and, well, you'll think of a way to fill all this space."

Enough said. This arrangement was totally unacceptable. It gave me an extra incentive to make sure my dad would be back under our leaky roof by the end of the day.

"I hope you don't mind, but I took the liberty of going to the supermarket to get all the picnic supplies," my dad said.

"I didn't know you knew how," I teased him.

"Funny," he said, patting me on the shoulder.

I followed him into the kitchen. There was a

refrigerator, a stove, and a microwave that he said came with the unit. Packages of paper plates and cups and plastic utensils sat on the Formica counter.

"I might need your help at the china store, too," my dad mentioned, pointing at the paper products.

"You could eat just TV dinners for the rest of your life," I said breezily. I wanted to give him an idea of what living alone would be like. "That way you won't need pots, pans, dishes, or bowls. Maybe just some silverware and coffee mugs."

My dad grimaced. I think the negative mental picture was coming through loud and clear.

"I'll learn to cook," he said fearfully.

"Good luck," I said emphatically. "It takes years to get the timing down in the kitchen."

My dad furrowed his brow.

"I guess there's always take-out," I added. "You could just eat Kung Pao chicken and egg rolls forever."

My dad shuddered. "Well, in the meantime, I've got roast beef and fresh bread for sandwiches. And I got mustard, because I remember that mayonnaise makes you 'want to barf.'" He pretended to stick his finger down his throat the way I do when my mom suggests preparing fish, cauliflower, or other unsavory items for dinner.

I giggled.

"So that takes care of our meat and bread groups. We've got carrots and celery for our vegetables." He held up a bag of carrots. "Delicious apples for our fruits. And then of course pretzels, sour cream–flavored corn chips, chocolate chocolate chip cookies, root beer, and an angel food cake to round it off. And what picnic is complete without cheese and crackers?"

I grinned. If my mom could have seen how cute my dad was being, she would have taken him back in a second.

"So what are we waiting for?" I asked. "You peel the carrots and slice some cheese. I'll make the sandwiches and we'll be set." I glanced at him. "You did get a carrot peeler, didn't you?"

"My first utensil," he said, holding one up proudly.

I used a plastic knife to spread the mustard and piled the roast beef high.

"Two is plenty, Ellen," my dad pointed out when I began making a third sandwich.

Plenty for him and my mom, I thought. But what if my nerves subsided and I got hungry? "Just in case," I told him as I wrapped them in tinfoil.

"Why don't you hang out and do some home-work for a couple of hours?" my dad suggested as we tidied up our mess in the kitchen. "We can go over to the picnic together."

Of course, that would fudge the plan. My mom had every reason to believe that I was going to be her escort. "Actually, Daddy, I promised Lila that I'd go help her out. She needs some extra hands to help carry the humongous luncheon."

"I thought that's what their servants did," my dad joked.

"Yeah, but Sunday's their day off," I replied. "So if you don't mind, we can just meet at the park at one o'clock."

"I'll be there," my dad agreed.

"Actually, make it one fifteen. Fashionably late." This would give me time to set up the picnic and make sure all my preparations were in order before he arrived. "And Daddy? Get rid of the beard. It's a bad idea."

He rolled his eyes and gave me another prickly kiss.

Fortunately, this would be my last visit, I thought as I left the cavernous space my dad called his bachelor pad. I just hoped he hadn't signed a long-term lease. Jessica's dad was a lawyer, and I knew a little about law from listening to him. I didn't want my dad to run into any legal entanglements when he moved out.

"How was Lila's?" my mom asked when I came into the kitchen.

The house was filled with the wonderful aroma of fried chicken. I had even smelled it as I came up the pathway to the front door.

"You just wouldn't believe the stuff that they're bringing," I said. "Full on gourmet." As you might have guessed, I had told my mom I was helping out at Lila's.

"Well, our little feast is all ready to go. We'll have leftovers till the end of time, I'm sure." She filled a container with potato salad.

"Let's bring the extra," I suggested. "I've been bragging about our picnic food all week, and I know my friends would love to try it out."

"Why not," she conceded, wrapping up some more chicken. "I dropped Mark off at Jim's this morning." She checked the wall clock. "We can head over to the lake in an hour or so."

I gave my mom the once over. To be honest, she wasn't exactly looking her best. Her blue and white striped pants and matching sweater just didn't cut it. "You aren't planning to wear *that*, are you?"

"I thought you loved this outfit." She sounded insulted.

"For a PTA meeting, maybe. This is a picnic." To woo my dad she would have to wear something flowy and feminine. Something that turned heads. "You should wear that flowery dress you look so pretty in." The one that I knew my dad liked. "And your pearls would be a nice touch, too."

"So dressy for a family picnic? I remember last year all the kids were in shorts and T-shirts." She patted down her sweater.

"The *kids*, Mom. And anyway, it's a little different this year. A little classier of an affair."

My mom looked thoughtful. "Well, I rarely have an occasion to wear that dress. And I've been so cooped up in the house the last few days. I suppose it would feel good to put a little effort into my appearance," she decided.

Man, was she easily tricked (not to mention oblivious to the plan).

Even though I was still a little nervous, I felt a glow of happiness. In fact, I couldn't remember the last time I felt this fabulous—as if I could do just about anything. Pull off an ingenious romantic scheme. Get straight A's in school. Hey, maybe I could even mend my skating outfit!

"I'm going to do a little homework until we leave," I said, heading for the staircase.

I trotted up the stairs, slipped into my room, and closed the door behind me. I removed the pieces of my skirt from the hiding place in the back of my drawer. I knew that *most* people at this point would have given up and used the material as a dust rag. But please, I was Ellen Riteman, saver of marriages, sparker of flames, preparer of sandwiches, and manipulator of parents. Yep, I could do anything.

I selected a white thread to sew the pieces back together. As I made the first few stitches, I imagined myself wearing the mended outfit, gliding along the ice gracefully. My friends must have been in the locker room or someplace, because in this daydream, I shared the ice with no one but my parents. My mom had an outfit matching mine and my dad had on a tux with a lavender cummerbund and bow tie. I was in the middle and they linked my arms. "Ellen," they said in unison, "we're a family. We'll stick together through thick and thin."

"Through thick and thin," I said aloud.

Eleven

"Mom? Why don't you go say hello to Mrs. Wakefield," I suggested after we had picked a spot to lay out our picnic. It was right next to the lake, underneath a beautiful weeping willow tree. Lila and her father had set up their elegant spread just a few spots over. They had come early so they'd be ready when the photographer arrived. "I'll get everything organized. I just want you to relax and enjoy the day."

"Don't be silly, Ellen," my mom said as she set down the basket full of food. "We'll do it together."

I bit my lip. I had to keep my mom from seeing any of the supplies I had hidden in my duffel bag. I wanted the romantic picnic, my dad's arrival, and the magical moment to come as a complete surprise.

"Look, Mom. You did almost all the cooking. It's my turn to pitch in," I insisted.

My mom looked reluctant. "And I'd love for you to pitch in. With me."

"Don't you trust me to do it on my own?" I pouted for effect.

"It's not that," she replied. "It's just that I'm happy to be here with you. I don't know how social I'm ready to be."

"Oh, look, Mrs. Wakefield is waving." I pointed down the lake to where Jessica and her family had set up camp.

My mom turned around. Mrs. Wakefield wasn't waving, and between you and me, she hadn't been. But my mom shrugged anyway and waved in their direction.

"It would be rude if you didn't go now," I coaxed.

My mom sighed. "Oh, all right, but I'll be back to help you finish up in a few minutes."

"How 'bout . . . fifteen?" I suggested. That would time her return precisely with my dad's arrival.

As soon as I had gotten rid of her, I got to work. I was glad I had rehearsed with the mock setup, because I knew exactly what I was doing. I spread the blanket out and flattened the edges. I put down the plates, the wine and glasses, and the white linen napkins I had dug up in the kitchen. I opened up the containers of food, tossed the fresh-cut flowers on the blanket, and placed the chocolate chunk smack in the center.

I stepped back to survey my work. I hate to brag (oh, why not, I had worked hard enough, I deserved to brag), but I must admit that I had created a masterpiece. It even looked more inviting than Lila's. Hers was more like an elegant wedding buffet than a charming lakeside picnic.

"Ellen?" Lila appeared by my side. "Hey."

I exhaled with frustration. I was in no mood for interruptions. The clock was ticking and I still had to light the candles and figure out how to get the cork out of the bottle of wine.

"Pretty cool, huh?" I said, confidently motioning toward my blanket. "Anyway, I'll see you a little later."

But Lila just stood there, surveying my work. "It is cool, Ellen. I'm really impressed. But um . . ."

"What is it, Lila? I'm kind of busy here," I snapped. "If you came for a compliment, I think I already gave you one when my mom and I stopped at your spot. Your outfit is perfect, and so is your picnic. The caterer did an amazing job." I put down the candles and lit them one by one.

Lila was just staring at me. What else did she expect me to say?

"OK, Lila," I continued, "your sandals are really beautiful, too."

Lila cleared her throat. "Ellen, actually, that's not why I came over. I . . ."

I turned back to the blanket and saw that the candles had all blown out. "Great," I grunted.

"Do you want me to help?" Lila offered.

"Oh, why not." I tossed her a book of matches. "Just don't mess anything up."

But as soon as I managed to light one, a breeze would blow it out. I was trying to block the wind with my palm when I noticed my mom coming back across the grass. I turned to my left and saw my dad holding a brown bag, on his way to my blanket.

"Thanks for your help, Lila, but you can leave now," I said abruptly, pushing her shoulder. "It's too windy to light the candles, anyway."

Lila stepped back and handed me the matches. "Whatever." She sighed.

"Mmmm," I mumbled, staring at the couple crossing over the grass, about to be reunited.

As my parents got closer to me, they became closer to each other. A simple rule of geometry that even I understand. I clamped my fists and tightened my shoulder, anticipating what might happen next. They were now in eye view. FDRP was about to play itself out.

"Hank!" my mom gasped, placing her hand on her chest.

My dad's mouth dropped. "Nancy?" he replied.

My mom slowed her pace and fidgeted with her hair as she approached my dad. If I had known she was going to put it in a bun at the last minute, I would have hid all her bobby pins. And her shade of rust lipstick suddenly felt wrong.

As I glanced toward my dad, I felt a pang of alarm. Of all days, why did he have to wear his dorky old plaid shirt, the one my mom tried to give to charity at least twice? And black socks with white sneakers? Hadn't he learned anything about how to dress himself in fifteen years of marriage?

"I can see you've resurrected your shirt from the dead," my mom said as she and my dad finally joined each other, a few feet away from me.

My heart was beating fast. Could she have meant that in an endearing way?

"This is a great shirt," he defended. "And what's with the fancy dress? Are you on your way to a dinner party?"

I felt my face heat up. It was probably just one of those backhanded compliments that my dad liked to give, I told myself.

But my mom didn't look like she thought it was a compliment. In fact, she looked pretty insulted.

They just need a little time to warm up to each other, I thought. After all, it had been a couple of days since my dad had left. It would take a while to re-kindle the flame. My plan was just a way to get the ball rolling.

"So," my dad said with bewilderment, as he noticed the picnic spread. "What's going on here?"

My mom's cheeks were flushed. She was staring so intently at my dad, she didn't seem to notice my picture-perfect setup. "Funny. I was about to ask you the same thing."

I knew I could have just come out and explained it to them, but I didn't want to interrupt the flow of conversation. The way I'd planned it, they'd put the pieces of the puzzle together. I had thought it would be really sweet.

"Well, I asked first. What are you doing here?" my dad asked, raising voice.

My heart lurched. He didn't sound sweet. In fact, he sounded sort of mad.

"Me? What do you think *you're* doing here?" she spouted back.

Suddenly I had an awful feeling in my bones. I took a few steps back.

"I asked you a question, Hank," my mom pressed. "If you're not going to answer, you can take your things, go back to your car, and leave me be. This is not the time or the place to discuss the legalities of our divorce. Although it wouldn't be a moment too soon."

"It's a miracle!" My dad flung his arms out in the air. "We actually see something eye to eye."

I bowed my head as I realized what was happening. My plan had backfired. My glitch-free, Jessica-like, brilliantly executed plan had exploded in my face. In all of our faces.

"And how dare you try and disrupt my day with Ellen. How dare you!" my mom screamed.

My heart dropped. My stomach sank. My palms

started sweating. My knees shook. Everything you hear that happens when something very terrible takes place was happening to my system. The world was spinning. I thought I was going to throw up. Or faint. Or die.

"Cut the histrionics," my dad retorted. "I know the way you operate."

"Operate? You're the operator!" my mom exclaimed. "Don't try and pin this one on me."

"Stop it. Please, stop it. Both of you," I begged as I ran toward them. I didn't have to look around to know that my parents had become the spectacle of the entire event. I was making it worse, but I didn't care. I just wanted them to stop fighting.

"Wait. I get it," my dad said to my mother, ignoring me. "You told Ellen you understood why she wanted to take me to Family Day. But all along you were planning to show up anyway." My dad glanced over at the pink blanket. His eyes darted between the wineglasses, the flowers, and the votive candles. "Did you actually think that a romantic afternoon picnic could mend all that's gone wrong between us?"

"How dare you accuse me of such a ruthless ploy." My mom's face was red with anger. "Leave."

"I'm not through," my dad went on through gritted teeth. "It just makes me sick to think that you would use Ellen as a pawn to get me back."

"Oh!" My mom threw up her hands in frustration. "How could you even think—I never—when *you're* the one who's acting so deviously!"

"He's not!" I cried. "And she's not either. Don't you see? This is *my* fault."

"We told you, Ellen, this has nothing to do with you," my mom said patiently.

My lips quivered. "But it does."

"It has to do with being trapped in a miserable marriage for far too long," my mom said in a shrill voice, glaring at my father. "It's just like you to pull this kind of a trick and then put the blame on me."

"Don't accuse me, Nancy."

"Listen to me!" I hollered so loudly that my throat stung. "I planned this."

"Ellen, don't try to be the scapegoat," my dad urged.

"I'm not trying anything. I—I—I'm just telling you the truth." I closed my eyes tightly, trying to hold back my tears. "I told you both that I wanted you to be my guests. I thought when you saw each other at the gorgeous setting with a romantic picnic, you could patch up your differences. I just wanted you to fall in love again. I . . . I . . . I wanted you to cancel your di-di-di-vorce."

My mom and dad turned to me. They both blinked, completely stunned. Then my mom widened her eyes, finally noticing the picnic spread behind me.

"Be mad at me. Punish me. Ground me. Please! Just don't hate each other anymore!" I said breathlessly.

"Ellen? Why? We . . ." My mom was at a loss for words.

I turned away from my parents—and saw that Kimberly and Jessica had joined Lila. They looked appalled. Instantly, I remembered what Kimberly had said last weekend after my fall on the ice. "One Unicorn looks bad and we all take a blow."

Well, I had done it again. Not only was I part of a broken family, but the whole school got to see my parents' final blowout. I had wounded the Unicorn reputation. I had embarrassed my friends. I had let everybody down.

I turned toward the Unicorns. "You guys are right. I'm the stupidest girl in the world. Don't worry. You don't have to kick me out of the club. At least I can do one ring tight."

"What are you talking about?" Kimberly asked.

Jessica looked baffled. "What's a ring tight?"

I stomped my feet on the ground. "No. I mean, one *th*ing *r*ight." I took a deep breath. "I quit!"

And then I did the only thing I could think of. I ran for it.

I ran at superhuman speed. I didn't know where I was going, but I knew I had to get away from everyone. I heard some voices call after me, but I didn't turn to see who they were. They were probably just taunting me, anyway. Calling me "ditz" and "Dumbo." I blocked out the noise and ran along the lake, into the woods, full speed ahead.

My wipeout on the ice had once seemed like the lowest moment in my life. But this was much,

much worse. The fall was an accident, but this was all my fault. If I had just let my parents be, it never would have happened. Plotting this romantic picnic was the stupidest thing I had ever done.

I hurdled over rocks and branches as I imagined what everyone at school would say about me and my messed-up family.

News about our picnic disaster would make the front page of our school paper, *The 7 & 8 Gazette.* Elizabeth Wakefield was probably out there with her reporter's pad and pencil, jotting down the bitter dialogue between my parents. "Ellen Riteman's Parents Go to War," the headline would read. If anyone had missed the showdown, they would read about it on the front page on Monday.

And Bruce and Peter would use it as material for their comedy routine. Bruce would play my mom, Peter would play my dad, and they would recruit Amanda Harmon to reprise my role.

"What are you doing here?" Peter would yell in a deep, manly voice.

"Me?" Bruce would mock a high-pitched squeak. "What are *you* doing here?"

"Me?" Peter would growl like a monster.

"Wah, wah," Amanda would cry. "It's my fault. It's all my fault," she would repeat over and over in baby talk.

This was the worst, most humiliating thing to happen to anyone, anywhere.

I tripped on a branch and fell. I pushed myself

up without checking to see if I'd skinned my knee and kept sprinting.

I ran on and on, nearing the far edge of the lake. But my mind and legs were losing steam. Just when I thought I might collapse, I came to a small boathouse. The door was open. I darted in and collapsed into an old chair, trying to catch my breath. I knew nobody would find me here.

Finally, I wept.

Twelve

What are tears anyway? Is there, like, a never-ending supply of them somewhere in your body? Or are they more like gas in a car—can you eventually hit empty?

I'd been crying for what felt like hours. And as far as I could tell, I wasn't anywhere near to running out of tears.

It didn't take a genius to figure out what must have happened at the picnic after I ran off. The police had probably shown up and arrested my parents for disturbing the peace. With order restored, all the families were probably having a blast and gossiping about "those disgraceful Ritemans." By now they were probably finishing up their lunches and getting ready to participate in the slew of activities.

In one week, my life had shattered. I no longer

had the two most important things in the world. Friends and family. It was clear that my parents' decision to divorce was final. And once they got out of jail, they would have a custody battle over who would get *stuck* with me. It was also obvious that the Unicorns wouldn't want me around. I was a total disgrace to the club. For the first time in thirteen years, I felt all alone in the world.

There was only one solution. I would leave Sweet Valley forever. I could go live with my aunt in Wyoming. My parents would be relieved to get me off their hands. I'd get a new name and concoct a new identity. I would make a new set of friends who didn't know about my checkered past.

But the thought of this only made me more upset. I'd spent my whole life in Sweet Valley. Every memory I ever had, every person I ever knew, every place I ever went. The Valley Mall, Casey's, the kids at the day-care center, Mandy Miller and her kooky outfits. I'd even miss Mark and Mr. Clark, the principal of Sweet Valley Middle School. And what about the Unicorns? Even though they'd go on having experiences without me, I would never stop missing them. The greatest times I ever had were with them. I buried my face in my hands and cried even harder.

"Ellen?" someone called out.

I was so startled, I nearly fell out of my chair.

In an instant I realized that Jessica, Lila, and Kimberly were standing behind me. I had been crying so loud, I obviously hadn't heard them walk in.

I guess they had come to make my resignation from the Unicorns official. "Wh-wh-what do you want?" I asked in a trembling voice.

"To give you something," Jessica said softly.

My vision was blurry from all the crying, but it looked like Jessica was holding a package toward me.

"Take it," Lila urged me.

I reluctantly took the package from Jessica.

"It's something we thought you should have," Jessica explained.

I stared at the salmon-colored wrapping paper. "I don't get it."

"Just open the package, Ellen!" Kimberly exclaimed, bouncing excitedly on the balls of her feet.

Finally I ripped off the paper. A million thoughts raced through my mind. Why are they doing this? Is it a gag gift? A T-shirt with a dead Unicorn on it?

The item that emerged from the tissue paper was the last thing I had ever expected. I couldn't believe my eyes. It was a skating skirt. *The* skating shirt. The very same lavender chiffon that I had mutilated on the ice.

"But . . . but . . . I don't understand. I . . ." I stammered.

"We knew you were majorly full of it when you told us you had fixed yours," Jessica explained.

"What made you think that?" I asked timidly.

"We know that sewing isn't exactly one of your talents," Lila admitted.

I felt my lip quiver. Were they taking a jab at me?

"Not to mention that you stink as a liar," Kimberly added, her eyes twinkling.

I looked from Kimberly to Lila to Jessica. They were smiling, but somehow they didn't look like they were making fun of me.

"We knew how much you loved the skirt," Lila said gently.

"And how bummed you were when you ruined it," Jessica added.

"So we pooled our money yesterday at the mall. But when we went to Leaping Leotards, they were out of them. We had to have a special order rushed in from Los Angeles," Kimberly said.

I wiped my eyes. I couldn't believe it. They went to all that trouble for me? "I don't know what to say. It's just, well, it's the nicest thing that anyone's ever done for me. I mean . . . why did you guys do this?"

Jessica nudged Kimberly, who nudged Lila.

"We knew you would be upset," Lila admitted. "We wanted to be here for you. To cheer you up."

"What made you think that I would need to be cheered . . . ?" I felt a wave of panic. Did they know about the divorce? Had they found me out? "Did you guys know about the, the . . ." Why was it so hard to say that word aloud? I braced myself. "The divorce?"

"I found out on Friday night," Jessica added. "I guess your dad called my dad for some legal advice. And, I mean, my dad wasn't tattling, Ellen, he just thought that I knew. And I think it was a pretty fair assumption. Best friends share these kinds of things."

I looked down.

"At the mall, yesterday, I tried to give you a chance to speak up," Jessica remarked. "But you didn't say a word."

"And so we talked about it and decided that I should be the one to bring it up to you," Lila said sympathetically. "Since my parents are divorced, too. That's why I came up to you at the beginning of the picnic. I thought maybe I could get you to open up. But you didn't really want to talk at all."

"Why were you keeping it a secret, Ellen?" Jessica asked. "It hurt *our* feelings that you would keep something so important from us."

I felt the tears start to well up again. "I never wanted to hurt your feelings." I took a deep breath. "But I was afraid about how you guys would react—that you might think I didn't belong in the club if you found out the truth."

"What do you mean?" Lila's eyes widened. "Why would we think that?"

"I thought—I thought you guys would think I was a total disgrace," I blurted out. "I mean, as it is, you're always making fun of my brain capacity and acting like I'm this huge embarrassment."

Jessica blinked. "We are?"

I groaned. "*Yes*, you are." Where were *they* that they didn't even notice how they teased me? "You're always calling me a ditz or an airhead."

Kimberly looked at me in shock. "But we—I

didn't know that upset you. I just thought it was like when we tease Lila about being a spoiled snob or Jessica about being the biggest living flirt."

I bit my lip. "But it feels more personal. I mean, there's nothing so bad about being spoiled or flirting. But being called dumb is like the ultimate insult."

Jessica nodded, taking it in. "I just never thought of it that way."

"And then when I fell at the ice rink, you rubbed it in. Like I was the lamest skater that ever existed." I looked down. "I thought if you found out that my mom and dad were splitting up you'd think of me as a total loser."

"Hey," Lila protested. "That would make *me* a loser, too."

I blushed, suddenly realizing what I'd said. "That's what I do. I say dumb things. I just don't realize it until it's too late to take back. I didn't mean to hurt your feelings, Lila." I shook my head. "No wonder you think I'm so stupid."

"Please, Ellen," Kimberly said gently. "We don't really think you're stupid. Maybe a little ditsy, but it kind of gives you character."

"Character?" I repeated.

"Yeah. Do you think we'd want to be friends with you if we thought you were totally without brains?" Kimberly sniffed. "We have high standards, you know."

"The only reason we tease you about being ditsy is because you're a good target," Lila remarked.

"And you're so funny when you get flustered," Jessica added.

"But if it really makes you feel so bad, we won't do it anymore." Lila tilted her head and grinned. "Well, at least not so much."

"You're just about the most dependable friend in the world," Jessica said. "I mean, what was this total nonsense about quitting the Unicorns?"

"I don't know," I said weakly. "I just thought you guys were going to boot me anyway."

Lila put an arm around my shoulder. "We wouldn't even be a club without you."

"We wouldn't?" I asked timidly.

They all shook their heads.

I looked at each of my friends, and suddenly I couldn't hold it in any longer. I started weeping again.

Jessica looked upset. "Oh, Ellen, I'm sorry."

I sniffled. "Don't be sorry. It's just that I feel so relieved. I'm glad that you guys finally know the truth."

"You know, there's something else I never knew about you," Kimberly said. "You're totally crafty! I mean, how'd you ever pull off luring both of your parents to the park?"

"Did you see the looks on their faces?" Lila asked. "They were totally stunned."

"And if I'm ever planning a romantic picnic for two, I might like some helpful hints on preparing it." Jessica wiggled her eyebrows.

"The flowers on the blanket were an excellent touch. Very springtime," Lila said analytically.

I stared at my friends. I couldn't believe it. They were actually impressed with me. Maybe it was just picnic planning, and clearly it hadn't worked the way I'd intended it, but I had actually outdone them in something.

But even if the Unicorns were impressed, I'd still be a laughingstock at school on Monday. "I'm just so sorry that everyone in the world had to see my parents have it out," I confessed.

"Hardly anyone was even there yet, Ellen," Jessica told me.

I sobbed. "You're just saying that to make me feel better."

"People always show up a little late," Kimberly said. "My family had just gotten there. We hadn't even set up our stuff yet."

"So you think I'd be overreacting if I moved to Wyoming?"

"*Please.*" Kimberly put her hands on her hips. "It's not like your parents were screaming into a loudspeaker. No one really knew what was going on."

"Actually, Peter and Bruce asked why you dashed off into the woods," Lila added.

I squinted my eyes skeptically. "They really didn't know?"

"I told them you were getting some exercise," Jessica said, flipping her hair. "Not bad, huh?"

"Peter said he didn't know you could run so fast,"

Kimberly added. "He was seriously impressed."

I giggled.

"I mean, everyone else was really too into the picnic to notice you," Lila said. "No offense."

I smiled. "None taken."

"We're really sorry about your parents, Ellen," Jessica said thoughtfully.

"I hope you guys realize how lucky you are," I responded. I looked at Jessica. "I mean, you have the perfect family."

"Me!" Jessica gasped. "I have the rudest brother in the world, a dad who won't increase my allowance, and a mom who . . ." She looked down as her voice trailed off. "Well, OK, I guess you have a point. I don't have it too bad, do I?"

I shook my head. "And I know you're still mad at your mom and dad for making you wear that T-shirt, Kimberly, but I think it's really cool. Your parents have such a good time together, they always do that kind of stuff. I just wish mine had . . . well, I always wished my parents were more like yours," I confessed.

Kimberly's eyes widened. "Really?"

"And, Lila, your dad loves you so much. He'd do anything for you," I said. "You live in a dreamworld. I've always been envious of—"

"But at least you'll still have both your parents," Lila interrupted. "You still get to live with your mom, eat breakfast with her in the morning, and make dinner with her at night. I never even see mine. Sometimes I feel like she doesn't care about me at all."

I raised my eyebrows in surprise. Lila had never opened up that way. She always acted like she was comfortable with her parents' divorce, never acting sad because her mom lived in Europe.

Lila and I met eyes. Maybe this was the beginning of a deeper bond for us.

Then Lila smiled mischievously. "But on the bright side of things, you can expect double presents, extra spending money, better vacations—"

"I'm sorry, Lila," I cut in, "but I don't think that stuff could ever make up for having a broken family."

Lila nodded. "Yeah, you're right. I guess that's why the Unicorns are so important to me," she confessed softly. "I think of you guys as my family."

I felt chills inside my body. I had never really thought of it that way. But it was true. There was something special, very special, that bonded the Unicorn Club together.

"Yeah," Jessica chimed in. "No matter what happens with your parents, your Unicorn family is here to stay."

As we shared a four-way hug, I realized something. Marriages don't always last, and neither do boyfriends or crushes. But when you have true friends like the Unicorns, they last forever.

Thirteen

It felt like hours had passed while I was in the boathouse, but when my friends walked me back to the picnic grounds, it looked like the activities were just getting into full swing. Jessica rushed over to join her mom for a spot in the three-legged race. Kimberly started warming up her arm to sink both her parents in the dunk tank. Lila spotted the photographer and waltzed over to greet him, primping her hair. As for me, I felt a rush of anxiety. I had no idea what had happened with my parents while I was gone. Had the battle ended or were they still having it out? Would my parents ever forgive me for what I had done? Would I be grounded for the rest of my life? Would they hold it against me every time I asked for something?

As I passed the central area, I realized that my

dad was nowhere in sight. My mom was still at our spot, sitting underneath the weeping willow. When she saw me, she stood up and waved, smiling warmly. As I ran toward her, my fears dissolved and a memory came rushing back.

When I was in first grade I came home with skinned knees and a scraped elbow. I had been playing Red Rover on the blacktop at school and had fallen on my face. (Some things don't change.) I remember the look in my mom's eyes that day. It was like she could feel the pain of the wound and of the embarrassment I had felt when I fell in front of the entire class. I had cried and told her that everybody was calling me a "lame dork" and said that they'd never pick me for their team again. She had held me tightly and brushed the tears off my cheeks. Somehow, I felt so comforted that I almost forgot about my fall. Being in my mother's arms was like a cure.

I don't know why as I got older I had stopped turning to my mom in that way. I didn't come home from the skating rink and tell her about falling, ruining my skirt, bruising my thigh, and feeling like I wanted to disappear forever. I didn't really tell her how I felt about the divorce or my own insecurities about myself. I guess I felt that becoming a teenager meant that you didn't need a mom like you used to. But I was wrong.

When I joined my mom underneath the tree, we hugged the way we had that day with my skinned knees and wounded ego.

"Oh, Ellen," she whispered. "I love you so much."

"I love you, too, Mom."

We pulled away.

"I don't know where to start," I said. "I mean, I have so much to say. Maybe we should just pack it up and go home."

She touched my cheek with the back of her hand. "What, and pass up this incredible picnic you prepared?"

"Well, I *am* hungry," I admitted, sitting down on the blanket. "Make that starving." I'd been too nervous to eat breakfast, and by now my stomach was growling.

My mom piled a plate with chicken, potato salad, and chips as I poured a cup of lemonade for each of us.

I looked at my mom uneasily as I took the plate. She didn't *seem* to be mad at me, but I could still be in big trouble. "Mom? I'm . . . I'm sorry I did all this stuff behind your back. And, you know, if you want to ground me or . . ."

She put her hand on my shoulder. "I'm not going to ground you."

"You're not?" I looked at her skeptically. "I mean, I know that the whole thing was dishonest and scheming and, come to think of it, pretty pathetic. But I was so upset about you and Daddy, I had to try something."

My mom smiled softly. "Ellen. There was so much love in what you tried to do here. When you ran off, your father and I had a chance to cool down and talk. We were both incredibly touched by your efforts."

I shook my head. "It was stupid of me to think that one picnic could fix everything that happened."

My mom's eyes filled up with tears and she dabbed them with the corner of a napkin. "I wish it could have. I'm certainly not happy about getting divorced. I'm frightened, Ellen. But your father and I have grown our separate ways. We had to do this. We really had no other choice."

"But where did it go wrong?" I asked helplessly. "I don't understand what happened between you guys."

My mom let out a long sigh. "It happened slowly. Over time. I can't pin down the breaking point. But it's important for you to understand that our problems had nothing to do with you. It was between us. And I'm sorry your friends had to see the worst of it. I never apologized to you for fighting in the kitchen that day when you were hosting the meeting."

"Yeah, that was pretty mortifying." I shivered at the memory.

My mom shook her head. "Parents profess to be these wise creatures, but we can do some pretty stupid things."

"I know a lot about doing stupid things." I giggled.

Grinning, my mom brushed my bangs from my forehead, then noticed the package next to me. "Hey, Ellen? What's in there?"

"It's a present from the Unicorns," I admitted,

cringing. I was revealing so many secrets today, it was amazing. "Want to see?"

She nodded.

Anxiously, I took the lavender skirt out of the paper and held it up for her to see.

My mom looked puzzled. "Isn't that just like the one your father and I bought for you?"

"Yeah," I said matter-of-factly. "Exactly."

"Well." She took a sip of her lemonade. "We can go back to Leaping Leotards and exchange it. A little outing to the mall might be fun."

"I'd be happy to go to the mall with you. But I'm keeping this." I exhaled. "See, last Saturday I was showing off at the ice rink. I tried to do this complicated turn and I wiped out. The chiffon frayed. I totally destroyed the skirt."

"Ellen!" My mom wrinkled her brow with concern. "Why didn't you tell me? Did you hurt yourself?"

I pushed up the leg of my denim shorts. The bruise had turned a sort of yellowish tone.

"Ouch," she said.

"No kidding." I rolled my shorts back down. "I should have come home and told you. The way I did when I was little. But instead, I hid it from you. I thought you'd be mad at me for being irresponsible. All week I sat in my room trying to repair the skirt on my own so you would never know."

"Oh, Ellen." She sounded hurt.

I touched the lavender fabric. "I'm sorry, Mom. I forgot that I could turn to you for anything."

She clasped my hand. "No matter how terrible anything is, I'm here for you." She clasped my hand.

"I guess I just needed a reminder," I replied.

"So how'd the skirt turn out?" she asked.

"Need a new dish towel?" I offered.

She grimaced. "That bad?"

I nodded sheepishly.

"You know what?" my mom asked cheerfully. "Let's just forget about all our troubles and eat."

"Good idea." I took a big bite of a drumstick. I had worked up a humongous appetite and my mom's home cooking had never tasted better. I watched the families fooling around in the middle of the lawn. Bruce and his dad were having a sword fight with branches. Mandy Miller was painting her mom's face like a clown. When I noticed Kimberly's parents drying off with towels, something hit me. Hard. I would never spend Family Day with both of my parents again. Who would I take next year? How would I ever decide? And what about holidays and birthdays and graduation? Stuff that had always seemed so simple had suddenly become confusing.

I studied my mom as she nibbled some chips. For the first time, I realized that she had taken off her wedding ring. Her hand looked awkward without it. It looked bare. And lonely.

But her bare hand said one thing clearly: My parents were getting a divorce and I would have to learn to accept it.

"Do you wish you hadn't ever married him?" I asked, still staring at her naked ring finger.

"No. No." She shook her head and looked me in the eye. "We had some wonderful years together. And most important, we had you and Mark."

"You're not just saying that because I'm your kid?" I demanded.

My mom took out the strawberry shortcake and cut us each a slice. "That's exactly why I'm saying that. You're an expression of me and your father rolled into one. You've got his sense of humor and determination, my temper and mannerisms. His blue eyes. My mousy brown hair and weak fingernails, unfortunately."

I took a bite of the cake. "I just hope I got the part of you that makes you such an awesome mom. I mean, this cake is perfection," I said with my mouth full.

She tilted her head. "You still think of me as a good mother even though I'm about to be a divorcée?"

"I'm lucky to have you, Mom. I mean, Lila hardly has a mother at all." I glanced over at Lila and her dad, who were being photographed in a canoe on the lake. "But, you know, now that you're single, I hear that Mr. Fowler is on the prowl for a woman." I wiggled my eyebrows.

My mom cracked up. "That would make you and Lila stepsisters."

"Scary thought."

When my mom laughed she closed her eyes and

squinched up her nose. At that moment, she looked more beautiful than I'd seen her look in ages. For the first time in months she looked happy and relaxed.

"I think it's a little early for me to worry about finding a new match," she said as her laughter petered off. "I need to do things for myself for a while. I'm planning to go back to school and get a real-estate license. And for a while, I think the person I'd like to be around most is you."

"I think that could be arranged," I agreed, resting my head on her shoulder.

"There are some incredible amenities here, El," my dad said later that afternoon.

I was at his apartment sitting cross-legged on the carpeted floor. My dad was leaning on a pillow that was propped up against the wall.

"Did I tell you about the pool and tennis courts?" he continued.

I grinned. "About five times now."

"Well, I hope the Unicorns know that they're as welcome here as they are at the house."

"Thanks, Daddy."

"It would really mean a lot to me if you'd hold a meeting here every once in a while. Afterwards you could all use the pool and the . . ."

"Tennis courts?" I filled in.

"And I promise that they won't have to overhear any ruthless fighting," he went on. "Unless I go crazy and start having arguments with myself."

I laughed.

"Next Sunday I thought you and Mark might like to go waterskiing on the lake. We could rent a boat for the day."

"Really?" I asked excitedly.

My dad clasped his hands together. "And since we've got the lunch left over from the picnic, we could bring the sandwiches and . . ."

I made a face. "Dad. That's sick. They'll have gone bad. They'll be totally moldy."

He laughed. "Just kidding, Ellen. Geez. We'll pack a fresh lunch—turkey sandwiches this time and a big fruit salad. And we'll buy a delicious and extremely fattening desert that no dentist in his right mind would let his children eat."

"Sounds great." I looked around the room. "But what about our furniture shopping? I think it's a matter of urgency."

My dad scratched his head. "We'll do that on Saturday."

It sounded like the most exciting weekend I had had in a long time.

"You know, I think this place has potential," I told him. I looked around the space, thinking about design ideas. My first mission would be to get rid of the chandelier. *And who really needs a dining room*, I thought. A Ping-Pong table, a Foosball, and a big-screen TV with a million videos and a laser disk player could transform the space into a very happening game room.

My dad got up and went into the kitchen. He returned with a bag of potato chips and a couple of root beers.

"Look, Ellen, I know I'm not the easiest person in the world. Not as a dad or a husband or even as a boss. I just hope that I haven't made you think that the male species is a real lousy one." He tossed me a soda.

"What do you mean?" I asked, opening the lid.

"That I don't want you to be afraid to fall in love when you get a little older. I don't want you to think you'll end up getting hurt. I'm sorry I set such a bad example."

I hadn't even thought of it that way. I've always had this mental picture of my life. I'll have some amazing job (we'll see how the apartment turns out, but maybe as an interior designer), a gorgeous successful husband, a house in Sweet Valley, two girls and a boy and a golden retriever. Seeing my parents' marriage fall apart hadn't shattered that picture at all.

"Maybe I can learn by your mistakes," I said.

"It's funny, Ellen," my dad said, leaning against the wall. "You never stop learning. School's important, don't get me wrong. But the life lessons you pick up along the way are what really rounds you out. I'm forty and I have a lot to learn now."

"Like how to cook and to clean?" I said knowingly.

"Exactly," he said, opening the bag of potato chips. The package split down the side and half of them spilled onto the floor. "Dinner," he said, pointing at them.

"You have some major education ahead of you." I giggled.

My dad looked at the pile of chips on the carpet. "So what do we do? A? Do we eat them anyway? The carpet *was* just cleaned."

I shook my head.

"B? Waste them and throw them away?"

I shrugged.

"C? Crush them?" my dad said mischievously.

"C!" I exclaimed.

"Then C it is." He bounced up and down on the chips. I joined him, making this incredible crackling sound and turning the chips into a pile of dust.

We eventually tumbled to the ground, laughing uncontrollably. My dad tickled me, and I laughed even harder.

"Stop it, Daddy!" I yelled.

I jumped up and ran across the room. I leaned against the window, looking at the courtyard down below.

"Hey. Did I mention the pool and tennis courts?" he said, coming up behind me.

I giggled again. "Once or twice."

I couldn't remember the last time I'd had this much fun with my dad. I guess he'd been tense around my mom for so long that he hadn't really seemed like himself.

"But did I mention that I love you?" he asked.

"Not lately," I admitted. "Did I?"

He smiled at me and we hugged for about half a second until he started tickling me under the arms again.

"Hey!" I exclaimed, dissolving once more into laughter.

Maybe my dad had moved away to an empty apartment half a mile from home, but the truth of the matter was, he was back.

"Ellen! Over here," Lila called out.

Lila, Kimberly, and Jessica were in the locker room, already changing into their skating outfits, when I showed up. At the picnic we had agreed to meet at the rink for our first ice troupe rehearsal after I'd spent some time with my dad.

"Hey." I put down my bag and pulled off my jeans. "My dad wanted me to extend a special invitation for us to hold a Unicorn meeting at his apartment."

"So's everything OK with you guys?" Jessica asked, brushing her hair.

I nodded. "The weirdest thing is that it's better than ever. I've never felt so close to either of my parents. My dad is letting me totally decorate his place."

"You're kidding," Jessica responded. "How fun."

"Yeah, I can't wait," I said excitedly. "Let's just say it'll be a challenge."

I slipped on the top of my skating outfit and turned for Lila to fasten the little buttons.

"Now, want to see the coolest skating skirt in the

history of the world?" I pulled the skirt out of my duffel bag and held it up for my friends to see.

"That is a serious skirt," Kimberly commented.

Jessica looked at the skirt in awe. "Whoever got you that must be incredibly kind, thoughtful, and all-around amazing."

I looked at my friends appreciatively. "You could say that." I sat down to tie my laces. "But I have a question for you. What exactly *is* an ice troupe?" The old Ellen never would have admitted she was clueless. The new Ellen felt fearless about asking questions that seemed a little ditsy. Especially now that I knew that ditsiness gave me some character. "Well?"

Jessica looked at Kimberly, who looked at Lila, who looked totally blank.

"So what *is* an ice troupe, Lila?" Kimberly pressed.

Lila sighed. "I don't know. Just, like, a group of ice dancers or something. I made it up. I thought it sounded chic."

"I don't know about you guys, but I'm not really up for being in an ice troupe right now," I confessed, becoming more honest by the second. "Maybe when I get to be a better skater, but for now I'd rather just have fun on the ice."

"You know," Lila said thoughtfully, "it would take a lot of time to make up the routines and everything. Maybe we can do it another time. My dad will still rent out the rink for a party, we just won't perform."

Kimberly shrugged. "Fine by me."

"Me too," Jessica said. "Why don't we move on to the next item on the agenda."

"Has this suddenly turned into a meeting?" I asked.

"Well, we have some important issues to discuss. We might as well get them over with," Jessica explained.

"In here?" The locker room was full of other girls, who were changing into their skating outfits.

"It's urgent," Lila said seriously.

"Do you remember the day that the three of us were talking by the drinking fountain?" Kimberly asked.

I felt a flutter of panic. I remembered it all too well. I knew they had been talking about me. I just knew it. "Yeah," I said tentatively.

"Well, we were debating a solution for the president problem," Jessica began.

"You were?" So they weren't talking about me after all. I must admit, in all the trauma of my parents' divorce I had completely forgotten about the president dilemma. "Well, the way I see it, we won't decide until we go to Sweet Valley High. Let's go on to the next item."

Lila shook her head. "If we don't decide, the Unicorns will fall apart."

"The three of us have been fighting so much over who's the best qualified. It hasn't been very good for club morale," Kimberly pointed out.

"That's why we decided that the best candidate for president would be you," Jessica announced.

"Who?" I looked from Jessica to Kimberly to Lila. They all pointed at me.

"Me?" I coughed.

"Yes, *you*," Lila said emphatically.

I folded my arms. "Very funny," I replied. I mean, even I wasn't fooled that easily.

"Ellen, this isn't a joke," Kimberly stressed.

I studied her carefully. She looked and sounded serious.

"You're the backbone of the group," Jessica said sincerely. "You've been concerned with club unity all along. You never stir up conflict and you never make an excuse for missing a meeting."

"Plus you ran the past couple of meetings so efficiently," Kimberly pointed out. "We were really impressed."

"And you obviously have a flair as a hostess," Lila added.

"Yeah, but . . ." I began, trying to dig for an excuse. But then the strangest thing happened. I couldn't deny it! I was dependable, I was organized, I was efficient, I was loyal. I, Ellen Riteman, actually had some virtues. Maybe they weren't as exciting as being a skating star, an expert flirt, or a talented actress, but they were definitely something to be proud of.

"So what do you think?" Jessica asked.

I bit my thumbnail. Were these qualities enough to turn me into a leader? I certainly hadn't thought of myself as the president type. But as I looked at the three hopeful faces staring at me, I suddenly felt a rush of confidence.

"Well, I know I wasn't born to be a leader," I said to them. "But I had this talk with my dad today. He says you never stop learning. And this week I've already learned a lot of stuff. I learned to accept my parents' divorce and I'm learning to be more honest about expressing my feelings. I guess there's no reason why I can't learn to be the best president the Unicorns have ever had!"

"So you'll do it?" Lila squealed.

"Yes! I accept."

We all high-fived.

"Hail to the chief," Jessica said in a deep voice.

I cleared my throat. "And as your new Unicorn president, I'd like to make an important announcement."

They looked at me curiously.

"Already?" Kimberly asked.

"Let's skate!" I declared.

Jessica smiled. "See, I knew you'd be good at this, Ellen."

"That's President Riteman, to you," I replied, and rushed off toward the ice.

"You know, it's amazing," I said in the locker room a little while later. I could have skated for much longer, but unfortunately the rink was about to close. "Just this morning I thought I'd be booted from the club, and now I'm president!"

"And now you're stuck with us forever," Jessica said, pulling off her skates. "You couldn't get rid of us if you tried."

"Yeah, that would be bad presidential behavior," Kimberly added.

"Don't worry." I laughed. "*Nothing* would make me want to get rid of you guys. You're the best friends I've ever had. And I'll be the greatest president. Only—" I broke off as an uncomfortable thought began to take shape.

"Only what?" Lila asked. "You're not having doubts, are you?"

"Not exactly," I replied. "It's just that, well, I just remembered what a great president Mandy was. I mean, I'm glad she still hangs out with us sometimes, but it's not the same as having her in the club. She still spends so much time with the Angels. I really miss her, you know?"

"I know." Lila sighed. "I wish there was some way we could get her to come back once and for all."

Will Mandy ever become a Unicorn again? Find out in The Unicorn Club #10, **Mandy in the Middle.**

A BANTAM SKYLARK BOOK

FRANCINE PASCAL'S

SWEET VALLEY

Twins AND FRIENDS.®